I0762253

The Witches' Couch

An Aussie Fairy Tale

By

Jonathon A McDonald

The Witches' Couch

First published: 31 October 2020

Published by Waltzing Wombats.

All characters and events in this publication, other than those clearly in the public domain, are fictious and any resemblance to real persons, living or dead, is purely coincidental.

A CIP catalogue record for this book is available from,

The National Library of Australia.

Original book cover and illustrations by J A McDonald

Book layout and design by J A McDonald

Editorial by L A McDonald

ISBN:978-0-6487961-5-2

-Dedications-

My miraculous wife

without her, this story would not exist.

And cheers to my mum. ***Thanks, Mum***.

To my endless sources of inspiration, in order of height, smallest to largest.

: I am the Destructionator; clean room must be ***destroyed!!***

: My name is Tiger-pea.

: The Princess and the Authority.

: Lightning Loguino.

: And a frog, who thought I should write a book.

The Witches' Couch

An Aussie Fairy Tale

By

Jonathon A McDonald

Table of Contents

Chapter 1 - The Veggie Jungle - 1

Chapter 2 - Storm - 6

Chapter 3 - Story Time - 14

Chapter 4 - Something Fishy - 20

Chapter 5 - Unexpected - 36

Chapter 6 - Boulders & Stones - 50

Chapter 7 – Kitchen - 64

Chapter 8 - Docks - 90

Chapter 9 - Before You Leap - 102

Chapter 10 - Homeward - 113

Chapter 11 - Somewhere, Maybe? - 121

Glossary 134

Biography of Jonathon A McDonald 142

-Note From Author – (well, *me*) 143

Review & Follow Me for New Books & Aussie Stuff! 144

Chapter 1 - The Veggie Jungle -

Just another Aussie summer's day: warm sunshine, an endless blue sky - and a kid named Squid.

Armed with his mum's trusty veggie basket, the Squid is on an adventure to explore the deepest, darkest, most treacherous veggie patch. Today he is THE GREAT NINJA ADVENTURER, AUGIE BARTHOLOMEW KETTLEBLACK, AKA 'The Squid,' and he is on the hunt for zucchinis and the elusive *golden squash.*

Dragonflies zipped by as butterflies flapped and flipped from flower to flower, and zucchini leaves the size of umbrellas jostled in the light summer breeze, hiding yummy veggies below. The Squid waded through the tangled mass until he spied a bright-green praying mantis among the foliage. Its claws twitching and snapping, its lime-green body swayed as it searched for prey. Its head swivelled from side to side, watching, and it looked right at him and lept! The beast's sharp serrated claws lashed out, but the Squid ninja-ed it! Diving out of the way of danger, twisting his body into a commando-roll, he yelled, "HAWWWAH!" as the beast's claws whistled past, missing him by just a whisker.

Down he went, rolling under the immense zucchini leaves, but the Squid found himself moving faster and faster. He had lost control - he couldn't stop! Down he went into the dark veggie jungle, tumbling and tumbling, crashing through the undergrowth. The vast green leaves closed over him, shutting out the bright sun and blue sky above. Plants and trees whizzed by leaves flew into the air as he tumbled. Then with a sudden ***thud!*** He stopped.

The Squid lay there and groaned, "OWWWAH-CRIKEY, I think I bruised me-bum!" Twisted vines twined around leafy dark green trees, bright green shoots breaking through the red, rich soil. His mum's veggie basket lay on the ground next to him: the Squid grabbed it as he rolled, startling a couple of silver-backed lizards, which scurried about flicking out their tongues and then, with a rustle, disappeared into the dry leaves. A kookaburra called out in the distance, its laughter echoing through the dark gloom, giving the Squid the spooks. He stood up, dusting himself off, and said, "No time for bludging. The Squid's got a job to do. Now, where are those yummy zucchinis and those elusive golden squash?"

The Squid wandered through the veggie jungle. Fuzzy yellow-and-black bumblebees buzzed slowly by as lady beetles whirred from leaf to leaf. Crunching through the dry leaves, he scrambled over thick, tangled roots and around bendy tree trunks. Something caught his ninja-eye, hidden at the base of a springy creeper: three perfectly striped, green zucchinis. The Squid ninja-jumped down next to them.

"WATAH! Ah, yes, the first pieces of the treasure," he said as he twisted the stems, snapping them off one after the other and placing them carefully into his mum's trusty veggie basket. "Now for the elusive golden squash." The great ninja-adventurer headed deeper into the shadowed jungle. Down the hidden trails, he crept, ducking through vines, looking left and right in case of danger.

A flash of purple in the darkness! The Squid froze; he didn't dare move a muscle. That flash of purple could only mean one thing: the deadly African broccoli. They hunt in packs, an extremely dangerous vegetable it must be avoided at all costs. They have uncanny hearing, and a single sound will alert them - then they ***EXPLODE!*** A zucchini slipped from the Squid's basket and fell. His hand flashed out like lightning: The Squid had caught it!

"Bloomin! That was close." He carefully placed the zucchini back into his mum's basket.

As light as a ninja, he crept down the trail, one eye on the African broccoli, the other on the jungle. Over fallen trees, through dangling vines, he silently trod. Finally, the trail took him away from the exploding veggies to the base of the towering corn trees. Their orange tufty heads looked down on him as their papery tendrils swayed back and forth, trying to snare the unwary. The great adventurer ninja-ed it, dashing through their leafy-tentacles he yelled, "HA-WWWWA!" Dodging left and right this way and that way, just one step away from being entangled – there, a clearing ahead.

The Squid sprinted for it; he just might make it. Powering into the clearing, he came face to face with the dreaded **PEAPODS OF DOOM!** They dangled above and behind him, their viney tendrils crisscrossing the trail, ready to entangle and poison their unsuspecting victims. Oh no! The peapods of doom had him surrounded; what a devilishly clever trap they had set for him.

(Peapod venom causes their victims to
gag uncontrollably and turn a horrible
pulsating green colour before they gasp
their final word, like
***"uU*GggghHHHhhhhhla ..."**)

"Is this the end of the great ninja-adventurer Augie Bartholomew Kettleblack? You can't have extra-cheesy veggie-bake without the golden squash buttons! No, The Squid must push on. No matter the danger! No matter the GggghHHHhhhhh-ness."

"Let's do this thing. ..."

The Squid stepped over the first peapod-covered vine - **ONE ATTACKED!** It swung right at him. He slow-mo style it - "HAWWW-YARRR" - swaying out of the way - *WWWOORRR-SHH - and* dodging the poison vegetables. Oh, the *danger!* Sweat beaded his brow as peapods chattered and jittered noisily at his survival: "*CHACHA-CHACHA-CHACHA-CHACHA.*"

There was only one way out: he would have to crawl through. Onto his hands and knees, he went, slowly pushing his mum's veggie basket in front of him. "Nearly there, nearly there," he muttered encouragingly to himself. Peapods of doom twitched and jiggled like a tremendous angry mob of summer cicadas. He glimpsed something: *is that a spot of gold?* Yep, there they were - the last piece to the veggie-bake treasure, the golden squash. Peapod venom dribbled down either side of it, glistening evilly. If just one drop touched him, it would be the end of The Squid. He slowly stretched his arm through the gap and grasped the elusive squash, twisting it till it snapped. Carefully he pulled out the golden vegetable; venom-pods shook and jittered angrily at his success.

"One down, one more to go," he said as he took a deep breath, calming himself.

There was just one more perfectly ripe golden squash ready to be picked, but it might be just out of his reach. So, out he stretched his arm, reaching and reaching. A peapod of doom hung near his face; Squid could smell the revolting pea-venom as it dribbled just a centimetre from his nose. He closed his eyes, squinching up his face, and reached; he got one finger on the golden squash, then two on the prize. "Just a little bit further." He grasped it, and with a flick of his wrist, ***OFF IT SNAPPED!***

"YES! I have it!" The golden squash was his. Oh, the mighty ninja-adventurer Augie Bartholomew Kettleblack was triumphant. The

Treasure was *his!* "We're going to eat well tonight! Yeah,we're going to eat well tonight!"

BOOOMMRRRRMM-MMM-MMRR_RRR..._

Chapter 2 - Storm -

Squid popped his head up through the garden vegetable leaves. Bugs and butterflies still zoomed about, but the sky had gone all dark with heavy, rolling storm clouds. Tucking the now full veggie basket under his arm, Squid waded back through the vegetable patch, through the overgrown grass and along the root-broken concrete path. Then finally, up to their little old farmhouse, with its flaky buttercup-yellow painted corrugated-tin roof and walls. The old hardwood floorboards creaked in spots - one spot even wobbled a bit - but the olden-timers had made it with love and out of anything they could get their hands on. Once Squid had snuck up into the roof to see what was up there. It was just old gum-tree branches holding everything up, with the tin roof slapped over the top; he guessed that was how they did things back then.

Squid's favourite part of his home was his backyard, with its rambling overgrown gardens; this was where his wild adventures would happen. Orange and lemon trees, a bopple-nut tree, grapevines, and an ancient green-apple tree, which all hung heavy with fruit in summer, and of course, there was the massive veggie jungle - you can't forget that bit. The backyard grass was vibrant- green, long, and shaggy and was great for hiding in unless Stew the sheep found you first. A couple of old tin sheds that lent in the direction that the wind was blowin', and a colossal gumtree towered over it all. Poss lived up there - she's a fuzzy ring-tail possum who loves the apple wedges his Nanna-Nan snuck to her sometimes with a pack of pink galahs up there as well and a family of magpies, who liked to dive-bomb the postie when she came by.

Then there was the old pine tree at the top of the yard Squid climbed it once, which wasn't a particularly good idea, as he found out; you see, when you do, you get all gummed up and sticky from all the sap. He had to sit in their old iron bathtub for what felt like hours, trying to get the darn stuff off; Mum hadn't been too happy with him. When he got out of the bath, he looked like a bright red prune with fuzzy blond hair. His sister Lilly cackled herself silly, but he didn't think it was funny. In summer out west, it gets really, really hot!

Nanna-Nan would stake out a claim under the big gummy pine tree - it's all cleared out underneath except for the pine needles and the chickens. Its thick branches hung to the ground, blocking out that scorching hot sun, making it all shady and cool. That's where you would find her, her feet plunked in a big bucket of cool water, sitting on an old swing seat she had dragged up there. She read book after book with a wet tea towel draped over her head. She said it was to keep her lid from overheating with all the words buzzing in.

And then there was Blue, a fat old blue-tongue lizard, who lived under the broken concrete path. Sometimes she would poke her head out when Mum came home. If Mum saw her, she would scream *reaaaaally* loud, thinking Blue was a snake - it's hilarious!

Squid opened their old fly-screen backdoor and yelled, "Lilly, when's Mum getting home?" plonking down his mum's full veggie basket on the kitchen counter.

"Later!" Lilly hollered back.

Lilly was Squid's older sister. She was sitting on Chester - their chesterfield couch. She was studying hard; she's had exams coming up for somethin'. When Mum was at work or Nanna was out, Lilly was in charge till one of them got back. She wasn't too bad, really.

Lilly could do a bang-up job of mum's cheesy veggie-bake. Lilly's fiery red hair was always done up in two thick long braids, along with a couple of forgotten pens stuck in. Her cheeks were splashed with freckles just like his were, but she was way taller.

"How *much* later?" asked Squid.

"Like, later-later. When she's finished."

"That's like forever away, Lilly."

"Yep."

"I'm bored."

"Really?"

"Yeah."

"Go back out and play."

"But it's about to rain."

"Really, Squid?"

"Yeah-ha, thick black clouds are all over the place, Sis."

Just then, a drop of rain hit the tin-roof. *Plop*, then *tink* … *tink-tink, plop-tink, plop*. Lightning struck …

CRACKBOOOM!

… which shook the cobbled old farmhouse.

"*Lilly!?*"

"*It's ok,*" Lilly quickly assured him, putting her schoolbooks away and taking the pens from her hair as she kept a careful eye on her little brother.

Squid didn't think it was ok; he was frozen near his sister. His eyes glistened with a hint of tears as he looked down at the wooden floorboards - he didn't like sudden loud noises much. They made him feel lost and all jumbled up inside to the point where he couldn't think straight.

"Let's have a look out the bay windows together at this bloomin' rain." Lilly carefully walked him over to the large windows which overlooked their yard, making sure not to touch him. The rain lashed down as the wind battered the darkened trees and garden; fruit and nut trees swayed; leaves tore off in the strong gusts of wind. A pack of galahs soared into the old gum, screeching their annoyance at the sudden tempest. The rain teemed down, pouring against the bay windows, distorting the world into strange blurry images.

"That's some serious rain, Squid; I haven't seen it like that for ages. No going outside now."

Squid was withdrawn and quiet as he stood there, not watching the rain, but then he asked with a sudden thought, "Lilly, are we going to flood!?"

"Nah, but the tide, she be turning," Lilly said with a sly smile as she looked down at her brother.

"The *wha*t?" Squid looked up with sudden interest.

"The *sea* lad - She be callin'," Lilly explained as she slowly reached out and wiped a forgotten tear from her little brother's eye.

"The sea? … But the beach is forever away, Lilly," Squid said with a distracted, thoughtful look. They had only been there once, when he was small, as it was so far away.

"Doesn't matter the distance; when the sea calls, she calls. You feel it in *here*." She placed her hand over his heart. Lightning struck again, and thunder ***BOOOOMED!*** Vibrating through his chest. His eyes widened as he looked up at his sister.

Lilly's eyes looked far away as she gazed out the window at the thundering storm. "Yes, Squid, the sea. She is beautiful with her vast, untamed waters, filled with the wild and things that are hidden".

"A story … really!?"

Lilly smiled down at her little brother.

"Yeah, Squid, why not? Mum said your old enough. We'll need some things first, 'kay?"

"Alright, like what?" Squid said excitedly, forgetting about the loudness of the thunder with all its crashing rumbles.

"Grab those two tea towels from the kitchen, and the broom, too, while you're at it. Then hop onto Chester while I grab something from the hall cupboard."

Lilly went down the hall as Squid tore-off to the kitchen. Lilly opened the linen closet doors, grabbed her pink polka-dot bed sheet, and headed back to the lounge room. She turned to their old and worn grey-green three-seater padded crocodile-scaled leather chesterfield couch, which they all called lovingly 'Chester.' Chester didn't look like a regular Chesterfield couch; he was definitely *different* - different than any old couch you had ever seen before. Nanna-Nan said he had just turned up one day when she was just a little girl and had been with them ever since.

Chester was slumped down lower on his right-hand side today: it always made him look a bit grumpy when he did that. He was facing the T.V. His warm honey-coloured timbers were carved with swirls and patterns, and his deeply buttoned overstuffed crocodile-scaled leather bulged with squishy, comfy comfort. And when you sat down on him, it was just like he was giving you a big warm hug as his three padded, leathered cushion seats squeaked and groaned until you, or he got comfortable. Each of Chester's buttons was made from some rosy cast metal, with silly faces moulded into everyone; some had their tongues poking out, while others were cross-eyed or laughing themselves silly or looking off in strange directions with surprised expressions.

And then you had Chester's feet. They weren't what you find on any old couch - not some ordinary rounded wooden knobs or stumps. You see, Chester's feet are what you call ***odd***. At the back were these two big stumpy elephants' hind feet. Elephant-sized, with their thick elephant wrinkles and big, shiny, cracked elephant toenails, they looked like they had just stomped their way out of Africa. Then at the front of Chester were these two big prehistoric-looking, scaled paws with protruding thick talons, cracked and yellowed with age; they were all sharp and dangerous-looking and a little scary with their heavy, over lapping blue-black scales - they looked, maybe, too much *alive*. Squid swore to Lilly that he had seen them move once, but he wasn't sure.

Then on top of Chester were Nana-Nan's six mismatched crochet cushions to make things squishier and comfier. They were blinding in colour, zipping from lime greens to hot-rod reds, with tassels of African violet and burnt oranges. Each cushion had something special worked into its pattern: leaping barramundi, wedge-tailed eagles, and Tassie devils hiding behind trees; starry nights, crashing waves, and the sun at sunset. Lilly loved that couch.

"Squid, pass me those two tea towels, would-ya?"

Lilly tied one around his head. It just looked like one of those bandanas that pirates wear. Squid's tea towel was sky-blue, covered in little yellowed daisies, with his blond hair sticking out the sides. Lilly tied her own Lilly's tea towel bandana was Aussie green-and-gold, with her two long red braids sticking out the back. Grabbing her pink polka-dot bedsheet, Lilly tied one end of the bedsheet to where the broom head was mounted. "Squid, pop this into the middle of Chester for me."

Squid grabbed the broom and waved the bed sheet about, and bounded up onto Chester, who groaned alarmingly; Squid tried to stick the broom handle in the middle of the couch, between the cushions. He wiggled it back and forwards, then sideways, trying to get it in. It just wasn't going to work; it wouldn't stand up. Squid relaxed his grip while he had a think. Just then, the broom handle suddenly sunk with a ***thunk!*** *Hmm,* he thought, *There must be a hole hidden down there*. He let go of the broom handle, which stood tall and solid, with Lilly's pink polka-dot bedsheet hanging down.

"Squid, grab the end of that bedsheet and tuck it in, please."

Squid bounced around on Chester, the couch's springs squeaking and groaning as he tucked it behind the cushions on an angle.

"That's great," said Lilly. Now the bedsheet looked like a real ship's sail.

"Ok, are we forgetting anything, Squid?"

Lightning flashed. ***BOOOOOMM!*** Thundered the storm.

"SQUEAK! SQUEAK!"

Squid jumped off the couch. "TINY!!! I'M COMING!" he shouted, dashing down the hall to his bedroom. He rummaged around for a while and then came back holding something. Squid jumped onto Chester and wiggled his way back down into the cushions; in his hands was a very fat and furry black-and-white guineapig named Tiny, shaking and quivering.

Lilly reached over and stroked Tiny's scruffy black-and-white Mohawk. "*Calm,* Tiny," she said with a smile.

"*Squeak,"* the little creature replied.

"You two get comfortable."

Just then, the flyscreen door slammed open with a ***CRACK!***

"What was that?" Squid hissed, sitting on his knees and glancing behind them.

A strong wind whirled through the house, picture frames clattered and banged against the walls, as loose papers flew up into the air and danced around. Lilly's pink polka-dot bedsheet billowed out, full of the surging wind; Chester creaked and groaned, his scaled paws flexed and stretched, his talons scraped against the wooden floorboards as his elephant feet bent and moved and tensed. Chester braced himself, just like a lion about to pounce.

Lilly began her tale.

Chapter 3 - Story Time -

"Across the cracked red land, over the broken Blue Mountains, and past the belt of green. The Sapphire coast - that's where you will find her, the Tasman Sea watching ever patiently. Wave's crash, salt sprays high from a coral shore, sailor's gaze out longingly. You might catch those sailors staring lost in memory over mugs of ale or hot cups of tea. If you are lucky, they just might tell you a tale or three. Far over the horizon, where land is just a dream, water is all that can be seen. The night sky is above, and below that is where the fearless must go.

"I once heard a tale told to me – the teller swore it was true. She said that she saw it with her own eyes and heard it with her own ears. A child was found far from land, who skipped and smiled upon the waves, who couldn't sink and sang songs of places not known to man who asked you to follow, or you'll be dammed. Lost places, lost things - islands with teeth. The strange and wonderful, and terrible indeed. With trees that sing and where fairies fly, there is such a place where the rainbows do end, and treasures fall from the sky but beware the leprechauns if you know what's best - don't hide what they think is theirs, or you will never rest!"

"Squid and Tiny, are you ready to lose your land-legs? Will you set sail on the fastest, mightiest couch the Tasman Sea has ever seen? Equipped with six cushion-cannons, a broomstick mast, and my trusty pink polka-dot bedsheet, do you dare seek the wonders? Do you dare face these terrors? Pirates look for the improbable, the incredible, the unbelievable, and the downright outlandish. So, do you dare?"

“Arrrr-alright, Sis,” Squid yelled as he jumped up and punched the air, with Tiny cradled in his arms.

“Squeak!” Squeaked Tiny.

“Then we have our crew. Tiny, the fearless guineapig, who can smell danger ten miles off. He’ll give us fair warning.”

“Squeak,” squeaked Tiny.

“Squid, the fearless adventurer who can find his way with no map or compass.”

“Arrrr-Arrrr”, Squid answered.

“‘Chester will be captained by myself. ‘The Red Lilly.’ Saltwater runs in my veins, and the crash of waves are in my eyes. Now, Squid, Tiny, the adventure’s about to begin - which way do we set sail?”

“The singing trees, the singing trees!” Squid cried.

“Then, aweigh anchor and set the main sheet sail. Tiny, nose into the wind and be on the sniff out. This storm is just getting started, and it’s going to get rough!”

At this, the little old house’s windows slammed open the curtains thrashed as the roaring wind and torrential rain streamed through, bringing with it thick milky mist, which hesitated at the sills for just a moment before pouring over, sliding onto the floor, and pooling and slithering across the hardwood floorboards to surround them.

“Lilly?”

The mist swirled around them, undulating. Squid quickly lifted his feet onto Chester, and so did Lilly. Something wet splashed his cheek. Squid touched his face as he looked up. The storm had moved inside. Grey, dark clouds boiled across the ceiling as lightning splintered and crackled above, jumping from light fixture to light fixture, blowing the bulbs *POP, POP, POP!*

BOOOOOMM! Thundered the storm.

"*SQUEAK!*"

Squid held Tiny tight in his arms as Lilly pulled them close, heavy rain pelting down and soaking them. Waves rolled out of the mist, breaking over the sides of the couch with a great splosh. Chester rocked to the side, his feet scraping across the floorboards. The water reached higher and higher till Chester began to float. Squid and Tiny looked over the side of the couch and saw Chester's clawed paws paddling and his elephant feet kicking in the water.

"What the?!"

Lilly's bed sheet whipped about as the angry clouds hurtled around them faster and faster, and lightning flashed and cracked till the house was no more. A great wave rolled straight towards them, lifting them up, up, up high into the chill, wet clouds - then down; they went sliding, crashing as the wave plunged.

"*Squeak-SQUEAK*!"

"LILLY!"

"HANG ON, SQUID, HANG ON, TINY … HERE WE GO!"

Chester spun, one way then another, down the crumbling swell. Lightning zig-zagged, strobing the storm-wrecked sea as waves smashed together. Hurricane winds screamed their fury, pelting them with iron-hard rain. Chester creaked and groaned, then popped and shook as he stretched, grew, and swelled; Chester's cushions catapulted Squid and Tiny high into the air with a *TWANG!*

"WHHAAARHHHHHH!"

"*SQUUEAAAK!*"

Chester's scaly armrests bubbled and contorted, first into the bow of a ship where his scaled paws spasmed larger and stronger, clawing at the air before they came crashing down into the sea. The couch elongated and morphed, forming a rounded ship's stern, where his elephant feet bucked and kicked, growing bulkier and heavier, frothing the waves around them. Squid and Tiny tumbled down; they hit the new deck with an "OAFF," an "*OAEK*" - and bounced!

Chester's deck was springy, just like his padded cushions sending them bounding and bouncing; Squid caught hold of the broomstick mast. Tiny landing on top of him with an "*eek.*" The sea roiled and rolled as towering waves peaked and fell; Chester churned through the surging sea, saltwater sprayed into the air. Lilly slid past them, smiling and waving with Nana's cushions, down to the stern as Chester climbed the rolling waves. The padded leather somehow swelled up, catching, and lifting her, as it formed a whole other upper deck, where a ship's helm sprouted from the black-green scaled leather, the wheel spinning. Lilly caught the wheel and held on as the wind and rain howled.

Old thick wooden rails flipped out and up around the decks; timbered stairs formed, one after another, clinking and clunking into existence, covered in Chester's strange carvings. The broomstick mast bent back and forth, shaking and quivering in Squid's hand. Ridged spirals rose from its wooden surface; Squid quickly let go in surprise and sat back watching. The mast grew, branching out, thickening, growing taller and taller, curving back and forth as it reached the storm-wrecked swirling sky. The broom head swelled and swelled until it formed a vast flower bud covered in thick, curling broom bristles; the flower bloomed, unfurling its odd petals - revealing a stranger vegetable-orange crow's nest within. Green tendrils spun from the mast branches and beams, racing and weaving together to form ladders and rigging, first down the mast throughout the ship.

Lilly's pink polka-dot bedsheet was at the top, flicking and cracking in the gale whilst the wind blew and blew; the bed sheet broke free and surged out, shredding into pieces and flailing in the storm-tossed wind, vine tendrils flung out to them, catching them before they could be lost as they bucked and danced. The vines reeled them in as they grew and lengthened, pulling the ship sails into position and securing them to the carved ridged beams of the mast with curly fronds of green. Now they had their pink polka-dot sails, filled to near bursting with the raging tempest.

Dark waves reared up and pounded against the side of the ship. Water crashed, sweeping Squid and Tiny across the deck, tumbling them over and over, spluttering in the salty water as the Chester rose and fell. Planting her feet, Lilly grabbed hold of the spinning helm, trying to wrestle *Chester,* the Spanish Galleon, under control. She stood proud and strong, her eyes the reflection of the stormed-wrecked sea; her red braids stirred in the gale as she guided Chester amongst the mountainous waves.

Squid looked up at his sister as he clutched the carved wooden rail with Tiny clasped tightly in his arms and lightning fracturing the sky. Lilly's clothing shimmered and morphed as he watched. Her white leather joggers turned black, flowing up her calves to form knee-high leather boots; her blue shorts lengthened into breeches; her little belt split into two and wove across her chest and waist, thickening to brown leather which jangled with chunky copper buckles; Lilly's white T-shirt *poofft* out with a *puff* as pearl buttons winked into existence down her now ruffled shirt.

A blazing crack of lightning and thunder crashed in front of them. Squid spun round and looked into the wind and rain - something black danced there. Was it a bird!? It whipped straight past him up to his sister, who caught it with one hand. In her fist, she now held a pirate captain's hat. Made of old black leather curled up on one side, it had a strange gold pin shaped like a lily with three long lyrebird feathers. Lilly placed it on her head … It fit perfectly.

"Right, Squid, Tiny," Commanded Lilly. "Secure those lines, batten down those hatches. Trim in that main sail. I will head Chester into the wind. Just us and the Tasman Sea now boys, and anything that dwells here - ***FOR ADVENTURE AND GLORY!***"

Chapter 4 - Something Fishy -

Chester, the Spanish galleon, rose and fell with each rolling wave whilst saltwater washed across his crocodile-scaled leather cushioned deck. Squid stood with his legs splayed wide for balance as the rain needled his face. He made his way slowly up the ship's stairs, his eyes huge and his mind awhirl with all that had happened.

"*SQUEEEEEEEEAK!*" squeaked Tiny, his little body shaking. Squid looked down at his furry friend as he squirmed in his arms; something was wrong.

"LILLY!" he yelled. "It's Tiny." Squid stomped up the stairs and over to Lilly, worried for his little mate.

"What's wrong, Squid?" Lilly said as she turned Chester's helm to correct his bearings.

Tiny twitched and jerked as Squids held him. Squid carefully laid his friend down on the wet leather of the deck. Tiny's black-and-white, furry, fat body spasmed and hiccupped; he had a very bizarre look on his face like he needed to do a - poop! Suddenly his fur started to grow longer and longer, his stomach bulged bigger, fatter, and fatter, and bigger still, and his legs and arms began to swell and swell, fat and thick. His whole body stretched out like a starfish and squirmed, like he had no bones, his body growing larger, longer - but his head stayed tiny! Then his ears grew, and his buck teeth elongated and expanded, sticking out from his mouth as his cheeks inflated. His head swelled and swelled. His eyes rolled round - and round, going cross-eyed up and down in opposite directions, then showing just the whites of his eyes until his head matched the size of his body. Tiny squinted up one spinning eye, as his left one found Squid and locked on him with a really intense look and, and, and … he - FARTED!

THRuPlppfffrrrrrr … ThuPPOOPTtt … rpfffrrtt.tt … Pffffff … ff

"Tiny, you … oh, bloomin' …" croaked Squid, clasping his hands to his face.

"Strewth, Tiny, what a gimassive fluff," Lilly said as she waved her hand around, trying to clear the air of the stupendously awful stench!

"*Squeeeeeaaak,*" Tiny squeaked in relief.

Tiny slowly stretched out his now-much-chunkier limbs as he got to his paws. He shook all over like a dog with an itch, his stumpy tail flicking back and forth. Squid watched, astounded, as his not-so 'tiny' friend slowly stood up! Standing on his thick hind legs with his furry black arms, which waved about, his chubby, white-furred belly jiggled while he got his balance. At his full height, Tiny was now as tall as Squid; and his messy black-and-white mohawk was massive. Tiny turned and looked at Squid with a smile, his brown eyes twinkling shiny and merry. Squid threw his arms around his friend as Tiny also wrapped his arms around Squid, squishing him in a chubby hug.

Squid looked over Tiny's shoulder at Lilly and asked, "What's happening!?"

"*Squeakily squeak-squeak!*" Tiny replied.

"Really, do you think so? Lilly, is that true?"

Lilly corrected Chester's course with slow turns of the ship's wheel.

"Lilly, what's going on!?" insisted Squid as Chester surged through a rolling wave, thunder and lightning continuing to crackle above them. Lilly looked down at her sodden little brother as the rain dripped from him.

"A *story,* Squid - you said you were bored."

"Story? STREWTH! But where's our house? What happened to Chester? Look at Tiny! We're on the sea, Lilly."

"*Squeak,*" Tiny squeaked as he ran around them on all fours paws and then stood back up on his two hind legs.

"You ok, Squid?"

"No, I'm not." Squid looked about. "Maybe … I am?" He stared wide-eyed at his pirate sister, Tiny … then back at his sister.

"Look at you," said Squid.

"Yes, Squid, look at *you.*"

Squid looked down at himself. He still had no shoes on, which was pretty much every day for him - he could run all day without them - but his shorts had turned into dirty-white three-quarter length trousers', ragged at the knees. His shirt had changed, too, into a blue-and-white striped knitted jersey; now, thinking of it, it was a bit itchy. But his tea-towel bandana was still the same, with its little daises, as was Lilly's Aussie green-and-gold one.

"Lilly, where are we?"

"The Tasman Sea, Squid."

"But this - this is no *story*, Lilly. We're really … really here."

"Yep."

"Really!?"

"Yep."

"Wow …"

"*Squeak?*"

"Ah-huh, *really*," Lilly said.

The storm seemed to have been listening to them and stopped its blustering. The rain eased and stopped as the swell slowed to a rolling calm. "Chester, take the helm for a while, would you?" The whole little ship bobbed suddenly in answer. Lilly let go of the ship's helm as Chester's wheel corrected itself, holding steady. "Let's take a walk, boys," she said.

Squid's eyes were wild. Lilly put her arm around her brother's shoulders, which he didn't seem to mind as she guided him to the stairs. Tiny skittered from place to place, his whiskers twitching as he ran about sniffing this and that. Tiny finally stood at the old wooden ship's rail, looking at the Tasman Sea. He had to hold on tight, as he was still getting used to standing on two paws. Then, together, they all walked to the bow of the ship, down the honey- coloured carved timber stairs and across the scaled, buttoned, bouncy, padded, dark-green-leather deck.

The clouds and mist cleared as Chester the Spanish galleon rose up and over, then crashed through, the rolling swell thrumming with pleasure. He seemed so happy that they all laughed and smiled in wonder as they gazed about; Chester was brilliant! Squid looked from the buttoned padded leather decks to the carved honey-timber doors, rails, and stairs. Vibrant green vines sprouting petite leaves formed the ship's ropes and ladders, twirling up the curved tree-trunk mast to the broom-bristled crow's-nest high above. Lilly's great pink polka-dot ship sails were all bowed out, full of steady sea breeze.

Chester had changed and grown to become a small ship - a pirate ship! Squid realised that Chester was just the right size for the three of them. Six cannons lined the lower deck, three on either side; Squid ran to each of them. *They must be Nanna-Nans cushions!* He thought; each had been remade into an iron cannon, but each was still as bright and colourful: lime greens to hot-rod reds, African violet, and burnt orange, with tassels of cast iron. And each cannon had one of Nanna-Nans unique patterns cast onto them: leaping barramundi, wedged-tailed eagles, and tassie-devils hiding behind trees; starry nights, crashing waves and the sun at sunset. The cannons were fearsome and delightful. Feeling giddy and dizzy with excitement, Squid whirled around, jumping with joy on the soft leather deck. He ran to his sister and wrapped his arms around her waist, hugging her with all he had.

"This is … BLOOMIN' AWESOME!" he exclaimed. "But, *how,* Lilly? He spoke as he gazed up at her and then all around him.

"Have you ever wondered about Chester, Squid? When you thought, he had moved, or a cushion slipped or bulged, in just such a way to make you perfectly comfortable? Did you think that was … strange?"

"It's Chester, that's … how he's always been. I mean, now that you say it - but *this*!? What is this?" Squid said as he gestured around him.

"This is the other part of Chester. If a teller of tales is strong enough, and if you are willing, things might happen."

"Does Mum know? Nanna!?"

Lilly smiled and laughed.

"They've got an idea. Maybe you should ask Nanna-Nan to tell you a tale or two."

"*SQUEAK! Squeak-squeakily squeak.*"

Squid and Lilly looked over at Tiny. Tiny had his guineapig nose held high in the air; his eyes closed, his nose furiously twitching and sniffing.

"Tiny, you smell something?" asked Lilly.

Tiny looked over at them and then ran to the ship's rail, looking out into the thinning mist. "*Squeak,*" he said before taking off, scrambling up the rigging, leaping from ropy vine to ropy vine, up and up the curved ridged mast, all the way to the bristled crow's- nest high above.

"What's that all about? Squid, head up the rigging and see what's got Tiny so sniffy."

"Aye-aye, Captain Sis," Squid grinned, saluting his sister and running off to climb the rigging as fast as a lizard drinks.

As he got higher and higher, the mast tilted more and more with each roll of the ship. Forward … down … back … forward … up and down … side … to side. Squid's tummy turned and flipped, then bubbled; he felt dizzy and sick, and then a *burp!* Puffed from his lips. He stopped climbing Squid, wrapped his arms around the vine ladder and looked to the horizon; it was the only thing that wasn't in motion that he could focus on; he breathed in a long, slow deep breath.

"*Squeak*?" Tiny was peering down at him over the crow's-nest.

"I will be alright; just give me a sec."

"*Squeak,*" Tiny said, popping his head back.

The salt sea breeze filled Squid's lungs as he closed his eyes and listened. The sound of the rolling water and the creak and squeak of Chester's timbers and couch springs settled his stomach; he took another deep breath and ascended slowly and surely, before climbing into the bristled crow's nest. Tiny stared intently out, his messy white-and-black mohawk buffeted about in the wind. He looked bigger and fiercer than he did before. "Tiny, what is it?"

"*Squeak, squeakily, squeak.*" Tiny pointed at something ahead through the clearing mist and clouds.

Squid sniffed the breeze: there was a smell. "What is that smell?" It wasn't pleasant; he knew that much. Squid sniffed the air again. "It's kinda like … " *Sniff.* "Yeah, old footy socks with …"

"*Squeak, squeak.*"

"Oh no … steamed broccoli!"

Squid and Tiny made the same *uUGggghHHHhhhhhla* sound as the wind pushed the smell up their noses. Squid yelled down to Lilly. "Something smells really gross, and it's coming from over there!" He pointed ahead into the oncoming wind.

Lilly strode over to Chester's rail and looked through the thinning mist as it streamed away in the breeze. There! On the horizon, a giant shadow in the distance - it wasn't moving; it was just there, dark and ominous waves smashed against the mass, sending white spray high into the air, then pattering down to the frothing sea.

"I think it might be an island!" Lilly hollered back. "Let's take Chester in for a closer look!" Lilly ran up the stairs and back to the helm.

"But it smells disgusting!" Squid protested.

"*Squeak, squeak!*" seconded Tiny.

"Boys, we're pirates, not wuss-bags. Now haul in that sail - we'll bring Chester in nice and slow."

Tiny and Squid climbed out of the crow's-nest and down to the vine-covered spar, hauling in the main sail and tying it off. The sea calmed, and the breeze lessened as they drew closer and closer to the island. The sun decided to peek out from behind the clouds, warming Squid. Legs wrapped around the big wooden spar, high up the mast, he looked out at the island - it seemed all slimy, and the stench was way bad.

"Hey, Lilly, it's covered in seaweed and stuff?"

"*Squeakily.*"

The closer they got, the calmer sea became, hardly any swell at all!? It was like the island wanted them closer. The island sort of stuck straight out of the water, with no beaches or any place to land; its sides were tall and wet and knobbly, encrusted with great sheaths of kelp that dangled down and swished about in the sea. The island was easily twice the height of Chester's mast and five times as long. The island rose high in front of them and tapered low down to the back. The stench of rotting old footy socks and over-steamed broccoli was powerful.

"Hey, Squid, is that a shopping trolley?" Lilly called up.

"Lilly, there's a jet ski!" Squid pointed.

Squid, Tiny, and Lilly looked about. There were chomped on surf boards, a rubber dinghy, fishing nets, crab pots with roped-coloured floats, and even half a canoe. Then, right at the front on top of the island was an oversized battered plastic Christmas tree complete with tinsel and baubles. They looked on in astonishment as solar- powered lights started to flash, and an old scratchy half-drowned chunky speaker stuttered to life, playing an eerie Christmas carol.

YOU BETTER WATCH OUT, YOU BETTER NOT CRY! YOU BETTER NOTTT-NOTTT-NOTTT-NOTTT ... Santa'S cOmmING-cOmmING-cOmmING, to town.

It was one of those big Christmas trees that they have at shopping centres with Santa. Squid loved Christmas time like every kid who knew about Christmas, but that odd Chrissy song gave him the heebie-jeebies. Chester slowly came around the island and up towards its great knobbly front. Squid and Tiny climbed down the vine rigging and out to the ships bow. Lilly joined them as Chester slowed to a stop. Stuck deep in the island's bulgy bit at the front was a grand, rusted ship's anchor, its old chain hanging down into the sea. Lilly studied the island - it kinda looked like a squinched-up, mouldy old face.

"Squid, it looks like a face, doesn't it?" she said.

Tiny gave it a good sniff: his eyes went cross-eyed, and his tongue stuck out as he swayed. Squid quickly caught his friend before he fell. "You better hold your sniffer, Tiny." Tiny clamped his paws over his nose, making his eyes refocus. Squid looked up at the bulgy, knobbly bits as his friend righted himself, "That bit does look like a big blob of a nose, doesn't it, Tiny?"

"Squeakily."

"And those lumps covered in slimy weeds - maybe closed eyelids?"

Lilly looked closer at the grand anchor; it really was stuck deep. "That could be a mouth," she said.

The island gave a little wiggle. The anchor's great chain, which hung down into the water, swung back and forth. Lilly, Tiny, and Squid took a step back and looked up. The large, closed eyelids were no longer closed. Instead, the island's mustard-yellow eyes peered down at them. Then the island smacked its gross seaweed-covered fleshy lips: seaweed and spittle flew into the air. The grand ship anchor and chain went jiggling, splashing, churning the water. Titanic-sized stained-glass crystal fins surged out of the sea, dwarfing Chester's sails, as the monster's mouth opened:

YYAAARRRRRRRR ...

The sea frothed with bubbles; the island thrashed. Its titanic crystal fins came down with a ***CRASH!***

Chester sloshed back and forth as the sea boiled. Lilly, Squid, and Tiny held on for dear life. "THAT'S NOT A BLOOMIN' ISLAND; IT'S A ***GIMASSIVE FISH!***" yelled Squid. The sea rolled and heaved, and a voice like thunder broke over them.

"TIDD BITTT, *YUUMMMYY!*"

"LILLY, IT'S HUNGRY!" screamed Squid.

"*SQUEEEEEAAAK!*"

"We've got to get out of here! GET UP THAT MAST AND LET OUT THAT MAIN SAIL!" Lilly yelled. Squid and Tiny sprinted, climbing the rigging as fast as possible, yanking on tied vines to release the sails. Lilly raced across the deck and up the ship stairs three at a time. She grabbed the ship's helm and spun it. "CHESTER, GO! GO!" she bellowed; Chester's sails filled with the wind. The fish monster crashed forward with a massive flip of its gigantean stained-glass crystal tail.

"... YOU BETTER WATCH OUT; YOU BETTER NOT CRY! ..."

An immense bow wave rolled off the stupendously sized fish, sending Chester surfing around, down, and away. With tremendous thrashes of the island-fishes tail, it propelled after them, making the sea churn and bubble. The fish roared as it gained on them, its yellowed eyes rolling wildly.

"MARrroo MARarr!"

Squid and Tiny jammed their hands and paws over their ears at the awful sound.

"IT'S GOING TO EAT US!" Squid yelled.

"Squeak squeakily, SQUEAK!"

"We're no titbit! BACK OFF, YOU OVERGROWN GOLDFISH!" yelled Lilly. "SQUID! GET DOWN HERE AND LOAD UP THOSE PORT SIDE PILLOW CANNONS AND GET THEM READY TO FLAMIN' FIRE!!"

Squid scrambled down the rigging as the monster fish gained on them, its titanic fins smashing the sea in pursuit. Its mouth chomped and gnashed in rage; its demented mustard-yellowed eyes swirled - then suddenly zoomed in on Squid as he clambered down the rigging.

"MARRURT!"

The sound blasted from the fish monster's throat. Squid slammed his hands over his ears in pain, his eyes watered, and everything went black for a second. He slipped!

"SQUID!" screamed Lilly as she watched her little brother fall.

"... Santa'S cOmmING coming ...."

Squid's world spun; falling and falling, he hit the ship's deck - and bounced! Then down he came again, sprawling on the deck, starring up at the curved mast, breathing hard and fast.

"Squid! You ok!?" shouted Lilly.

Squid quickly checked himself, patting himself all over, "Nothin' broken!" he called up to his sister smiling.

"*SQUEAK!*" Tiny yelled. The monster fishe's mouth slammed down, just missing Chester. Saltwater sprayed into the air. Chester, the Spanish galleon, was hammered to the side and then tipped. Squid went sliding across the leather deck, knocking over a pile of cushioned coloured cannon balls.

"GET THOSE PORT-SIDE CANNONS LOADED!" commanded Lilly.

Squid scrambled about stuffing cushion cannonballs into the three port-side cannons. "READY, CAPTAIN" he yelled.

"*Squeak, SQUEEEEEEEEEEEAAAAAAK!*"-

"MARAH MARAHOOOT!"

The fish monster charged with great smashes of its gargantuan crystal tail and titanic stained-glass fins. Its mouth opened impossibly wide - all they could see was its gross squirmy orange tongue wiggling at them and its flared nostrils quivering. The bent plastic Christmas tree at the top jingled about as the gimassive fish monster charged forward, ready to swallow them whole.

"... YOU BETTER NOTTT-NOTTT-NOTTT-NOTTT ..."

"Break to port, BREAK TO PORT!" Lilly spun the ship's wheel hard.

Chester the Spanish galleon swung, swaying wildly, and broadsided the monstrosity. Tiny was thrown from the crow's-nest, falling, tumbling. "*SQUEEEAK!*" Tiny yelled as he fell. He stretched out a paw, catching hold of the vine just before he plunged into the heaving sea. Chester rocked back, zipping Tiny around and swinging him right over the top of the charging monster. As he whizzed over the creature's head, Tiny stuck out his tongue and blew a big fat raspberry at it:

"THRULPULPULPULPULPUPPUP!"

The fish monster's mustard-yellow eyes swirled with anger and hunger as Squid looked down the throat of the charging beast.

"***FIRE THE PILLOW CANNONS!!***" commanded Lilly.

Squid smiled mischievously and pulled the firing cord, saying, "*Merry Christmas, Bubbles.*"

BOOM! ... BOOM! ... BOOM!

Two pillow cannonballs went sailing straight down thef i s h monster's gullet. The other went straight up its … left nostril?!

The colossal fishy creature sloshed to a stop and smacked down its giant gob, squinching its mouldy old seaweed face up tight. Green and pink smoke drifted from the corners of its mouth as the creature rolled side to side in the sea. Its crazy mustard-yellow eyes swirled its gross blob of a nose twitched and sniffed.

"Hey, Squid, are they feathered cannon balls?" Lilly asked.

"Yeah, Sis, I think they are."

"Oh no …"

"*Squeak, SQUEAK.*"

"Everybody, *GRAB ONTO SOMETHING!*"

The gimassive fish monster started to SNIFF … to SNUFFLE, … to …

AH … AHHHH …

AHHHHHHH …

CHOOO!

The sneeze hit them like a hurricane with a cricket bat. Chester blasted off in a flurry of fish boogies. Lilly, Squid, and Tiny screamed and yelled, holding on for dear life as Chester bounced and skipped across the top of the waves, racing over the Tasman Sea and leaving the crusted seaweedy fish monster … hungry.

Chapter 5 - Unexpected -

Squid lay on the deck and looked up at a clear blue sky. He felt gooey. Yeah, that's it – wet, gloopy and gooey. It was a weird feeling. He sat up. "What the …?" Chunky greenie-yellowed globs of goo dripped from the ropes and rigging; it squelched and plopped as it slid onto the deck.

"This is SO GROSS!!" yelled Lilly as she wiped goo from her eyes and face. She had ended up not far from Squid, her back against a crimson cannon. Tiny was upside down between them.

"*Squeak.*" Tiny shook himself all over, showering Squid and Lilly with goober-chunks.

"TINNNNY, seriously! Couldn't you have done that somewhere else!?" Lilly cried.

"*Sque-sque-sque,*" he giggled.

Squid and Lilly tried to stand, but they slipped and slid in the chunky goo; quickly, they grabbed Chester's rail tokeep from falling over.

"What is this stuff?" Squid asked as he squished it through his fingers.

"*Squeak.*"

"Yes, Tiny, I think you're right … fish boogers," Lilly agreed.

"*Yarrruck ugggghhhhhhhh* ... gross, the stuff's everywhere," squirmed Squid as he flicked his hands, shaking greenish-yellow globs from them.

Chester started shaking from his bow to his stern, like a wet dog, bouncing them up and down. The tree mast went flinging side to side. The deck rippled and twisted in rolling waves, sending Tiny, Lilly, and Squid bouncing around the leather-padded deck.

"WOAH, CHESTER, WOOOAH!" called Lilly.

Squid and Tiny just laughed and jumped higher and higher as if they were on some big blow-up jumping castle. The ship's wheel spun one way and the other, shooting boogers off into the air. Vine ropes and rigging whipped and cracked, spraying globs of goo and plopping them into the sea, leaving Chester calm and spotless. Squid's bounce became a walk as the leather deck firmed up under his feet. He headed to the ship's rail, wiping the remaining boogers from his face and flicking them over the side.

"Where are we?" Squid said.

Lilly walked over to Chester's rail and looked out with him; sapphire-blue waves, as clear as glass, rolled up onto a pristine white-sandy shore. Chester had become beached high on the sandbank with half his keel out of the water. The place was surrounded by light red-and-orange sandstone, which rose up in a wall all around them. Salt-stunted trees and odd-shaped rock pools dotted the sides of the cove, glistening in the warm sun.

"Wow, how cool is this place? It reminds me of when you were just a little tacker when we went to the south coast together." Lilly said.

"Really? I sorta remember. I'm goin' for a swim - that water looks awesome!" Squid cried.

"*Squeak!*" second Tiny.

The three pirates ran to Chester's bow, where a rope ladder unfurled with a clatter; it had wooden steps tied into it, which made coming and going much, much easier. "Thanks, Chester," said Lilly as she clambered down and jumped onto the sandy shore.

They all played on the beach, even Chester, as his bow was so high out of the water. His great clawed paws were able to help Lilly build a sandcastle on the beach. Chester pushed and mounded the sand as Lilly added the details; soon, they had created a castle that rivalled all sandcastles before it. Thick-walled battlements circled three mighty sandy towers, which reached up high into the air at its centre. Squid and Tiny scampered around collecting seashells, little stones and long strands of dark seaweed, which they ran back to the construction site. Carefully they added the coastal decorations till the sandcastle sparkled in the light.

Chester brushed his hefty, scaled paws together, knocking the sand from them, a tell-tale sign of a job done. Lilly, Tiny, and Squid stood back and admired their work as a wave rolled up the beach, filling the sandy moat and sluicing around the magnificent castle.

"That loo ..." Lilly was about to say as Chester's elephant foot stomped and *kicked!* Sending salty-water surging forwards, sloshing and drenching them all. "CHESTER!" Lilly cried.

Squid and Tiny laughed their butts off as Chester giggled and giggled with vibrating quakes and wobbles. The ship rolled to his side and stretched out his great scaled paws, mounding and moulding the sand into a type of backrest for his bow as his bulky grey elephant feet slowly paddled in the slight surf; Chester relaxed in the sun.

Tiny, Lilly, and Squid decided to go for a walk to dry off along the time smoothed sandstone. Rock pools glistened in the summer light, each a window into a little ocean world where red-clawed crabs scuttled about and yellow-and-blue striped fish zipped around. The pirates touched strange sea anemones with their sticky tentacles, which sucked at their fingers, and they watched bulbous-shelled seasnails slowly mosey their way along.

The Aussie sun was hot, and shade was desperately needed, so they went up the beach, seeking shelter under the salt-stunted trees; that's where Squid spotted something.

"There's a trail!"

"What, Squid?"

"*Squeak?*"

"I found a Trail," Squid called back to them.

"Really?" Lilly said.

"Yeah, I'm looking at it!"

Lilly walked towards Squid and Tiny. "Well, let's find out where it goes then; hey, squirt!"

"I know you are, but what am I?" he called back to his sister, who smiled and stuck out her tongue, pulling a funny face at him. Squid laughed as he and Tiny scampered along the track.

The sandy path took them away from the beach through the twisted trees. Lilly trailed along not too far behind them. The trail led them up the steep sandstone bushy bluff, where seagulls floated about in the wind squawking their annoyance at the sudden appearance of trespassers. Chester looked relatively small down there, lazing on the beach with them so high; the sapphire-blue Tasman Sea stretched far behind him, glittering in the warm sun. So, up and up, the three pirates puffed, pushing on till they got to the very top. What they saw when they got there was … unreal!

Metallic shimmering trees filled the valley before them: blues, pinks, scarlets, and spots of lavender dazzled them. The sea breeze wove across the forest canopy, twisting and turning the strange shining leaves, their colours flickering from dark to light and light to dark. Aussie black cockatoos flew over the treetops with long streamers of blue-black feathers, calling out in a wondrous screeching melody. A broken granite tooth of a mountain rose in the distance, surrounded by the glinting metallic forest and rounded emerald-green rolling hills.

The group stood there, mouths open, struck dumb by what lay before them. The rocky trail they had climbed continued down the other side - down to the strange forest below.

"LET'S GO!" shouted Squid, scrambling down the path. Tiny was fast on his heels.

Lilly stood there momentarily, looking in bewilderment, then ran after them. The forest softly tinkled and chimed as the wind danced among the metallic leaves. The strange trees had chunks of silver for bark, which seemed to glitter and glow with their own light; their limbs were gracefully curved and pruned to perfection. Fat yellow-and-blue-dotted toad stools and frilly pink mushrooms poked up all over the place. Each tree was marvellous in its colour, and all were arranged in perfect symphony with each other.

Great boulders were dotted about the forest, bedded down in the thick green moss, with the strange trees growing over or around them, their thick, strong roots hugging them tightly. The boulders all seemed to be angled and placed in specific spots so that all looked their absolute best, all cleaned and polished. Others looked to defy gravity, balanced one on top of the other. Some had even been arranged to form immense stone gateways, framing the perfect picture of the painted metallic forest beyond.

Curly ferns swayed back and forth in the light sea breeze as little streams trickled in and out around boulders and the trees and then cascaded into clear pools filled with water-smoothed coloured pebbles. Wee fish darted about in the water, and bright green frogs sprung from bendy cattail reeds, plopping into the mirrored waters. It was dreamlike, perfect, and wild.

Lilly looked up at a great, scarlet-leafed tree, its leaves tinkling delightfully in the gentle wind. She smiled, filled with a sense of happiness, and slowly reached out, placing her hand against its silvery, chunky bark … Music burst forth! Lilly jerked her hand away and looked around - the music slowly faded and then stopped. Puzzled, she looked at her tingling hand and then back up at the scarlet-leafed tree.

"What was that?" asked Squid.

"*Squeak?*"

Lilly slowly reached back out again, placing her hand against the tree music burst forth, vibrating and tingling through her. "That's

DISCO! That music Nanna-Nan plays really loud," smiled Squid. They laughed with surprise as they all looked about with curiosity.

"Squid, check that one," instructed Lilly, pointing at a deep-purple-crowned tree.

"Ok, Sis." Squid skipped and jumped over a stream and hugged the tree. A deep soul tune rolled out. "Whhhaaaattt-t-t?" Squid leapt back, with his teeth chattering, his whole-body reverberating. Shaking off the vibrations, Squid wiggled his tongue, "erllalalala," and smiled; slowly this time, he reached out and placed his hand against the tree. A woman's warm, sassy voice sang out. Squid looked up at the beautiful tree and smiled delightedly. He looked to the others, who smiled back. "Lilly, it's the singing trees!" he exclaimed.

They raced off in every direction, trying this one and that one; music blared, tinkled, and strummed, rolling and washing all around them. Tiny started jumping up and down on the roots of a giant emerald tree. "*Squeakily squeak ... Squeak.*" Scottish bagpipes squawked and shrilled out with stops and starts.

The pirates played for a while, wandering throughout the forest until they stumbled into a sunlit clearing. A couple of over-large lounging boulders greeted them; thick green moss crept up their sides, and two old, gnarled singing trees clung precariously high above. The soft chime of their pink-and-purple metallic leaves relaxed them, so the pirates decided to have a break from their play. Lilly got comfy and sat with her back against the sun-warmed stone, pushing her captain's hat down over her eyes. Tiny and Squid clambered up the boulders to the very top, where they sat swinging their feet and looking about the painted forest.

Squid relaxed. He finally had a chance to take everything in; his life had gotten a whole lot more interesting, he pinched his arm till the skin went white, then pink, and then he twisted it. “OH! Flippin.” It *hurt* - that meant … He wasn’t dreaming. He smiled, rubbing his arm, perched next to his much larger than his regular furry friend, who seemed to be sniffing at the air. Tiny turned his head, sniffing and sniffing.

“*Squeak?*”

Squid started sniffing, too - there was something. Something that smelt … yum! “You know what that smells like, Tiny?”

“*Squeak!*”

"One of Mum’s, mmmmm-yum apple pies.”

“Hey, Lilly?” he called.

“Yeah, Squid?”

“Can you smell that?”

Lilly flicked up her hat and opened her eyes; she looked around and sniffed at the air. It smelt just like one of Mum’s cinnamon myrtle deep-pan apple pies. And there it was! Just floating in the bloomin’ air at the edge of the forest.

“*Squeak, squeakily!*” Tiny had spotted the floating dessert, too.

“Oi, you two. Scamper on down here, would ya?” Tiny and Squid climbed on down and joined Lilly. The three pirates kept a close eye on that yummy scrummy pie. “Alright, pirates, it’s not every day a pie just wanders on up on ya and wants to be eaten. So, I’ll go left; Squid, you go right. That leaves you, Tiny. You head straight up the middle, and we'll grab that pie, 'kay? Ready, get set, *CHARGE!*" yelled Lilly. They ran for that pie. They were just about to grab it - when it took off! Zipping off through the forest, "It's getting away! Come on, you scallywags, you can move faster than that," called Lilly. They chased the pie up and over boulders along curved silvered trees through the forest they went, hopping and jumping over trickling streams, chasing that pie; they slipped, and they slid as the tempting dish zipped this way and that. Up and around, then finally down, the three pirates had it cornered, nowhere for that pie to zip or slip; the hungry pirates closed in. "All right, pie, you put up a good fight, but it's time to be eaten," Lilly panted, huffing and puffing.

"*He-he-he,*" giggled the pie.

"Squid, did that pie just laugh at me?"

"Well, yeah … ? It did, Lilly."

"Well, then, I'm having the first bite!"

"You can't eat me!" said the pie.

"Yes, I can; you're a *pie*."

"Am I?"

"You look like a pie and smell like a yummy scrummy pie … You're a pie."

"Really? Well, the name's Apple, but I'm still not a pie … Ha!" with a giggle and a hiccup, the pie burst into a ball of sparkly green smoke. Then something coughed and gagged as the smoke slowly cleared, leaving a fairy in the air … A very strange-looking kid-sized fairy. It had Granny-Smith green-apple skin, long spiky bright orange hair, and these big purple eyes. He wore a little black leather jacket and leather pants with rainbow spikes sticking out all over the place, with a steel chain belt wrapped around his waist. Black-felt butterfly wings flapped and flipped, shimmering in the light; he hovered in front of them and, with a cheeky smile, said, "Ha, got you! Got you, pirates, Ha … thought I was pie, ha!" The fairy smiled with its hands on its hips, looking proud of itself. Tiny ran and leapt, catching the fairy and pinning him to the ground.

"*Squeak.*"

"Ha, pirates got you, got you. Still might *taste* like pie!" Lilly said as she walked over and smiled down at the fairy.

"No ... No, don't eat me! Get your darn lion off me!" shouted and squirmed the fairy.

"You hold him still, Tiny," replied Lilly.

"*Squeak.*" squeaked Tiny.

"What you want, you darn stinking pirates!?" the fairy squawked.

"We're hungry, and you made us work up quite a bit of an appetite with all that running around you had us doing."

"Got nothing for you, you - stinking pirates."

"I don't know about that … We could still eat … you!"

"*Squeak, squeak,*" said Tiny as he started licking the fairy's face all over.

"Hold up a minute ... Yuck! Just wait …That's gross … a moment, stop … you darn lion … **STOP LICKING ME!**"

"Tiny, let him speak." Lilly giggled.

"*Squeak.*"

"Ok, ok … you want food, yeah? I know where there is much better food than … than me!"

Tiny licked him again.

"It's not far … *really*!"

"Ok, but if you're lying ... Tiny here might just have to have a snack of some *fairy legs*."

Squid whispered to Lilly.

"You're not serious, are you?"

"No, Squid, just keeping him honest."

They followed the strange fairy as he fluttered and flitted to a trail that snaked its way through the forest.

"So, how long have you lived here, fairy?" asked Squid.

"Name's Apple."

"All right, Apple, I'm Squid. That's my sis Lilly, and that lion's Tiny."

"Well, nice to meet-cha …" Apple said as he gave Squid a quizzical look; "You're not too bad for pirates, maybe a little on the short side, and not so furry except that lion of yours."

"Thanks … I think," Squid replied.

"So, how long?" Squid asked.

"Well, forever, I was born atop that big amaranth tree over there: she's my mum loves punk rock, really gets swaying when a storm's a-blowin'. Dad's a Ficus. He plays the panpipes; he's all mysterious; that's how he landed mum. Those boulders over there call themselves the 'Rolling stones' how original! I must admit, that one in the middle's got some serious moves. Last winter solstice, this place was *rocking*. Aurora turned up and put on a wicked light show; the Red Daisies laid down a fat beat, which got everybody *jumpin'*. Then the trees lit up! It was like, just … damn! Just, you know, man, like … ***bounce!*** Any-who, here we are."

"It's a small cave," said Lilly looking over at Squid and thinking this Apple might be a bit cray-cray.

"Yeah, well, head on in; it opens up."

"I think you should go first," said Lilly. Tiny gave Apple's wings a good sniff.

"Ok, ok, keep your leaves on. Back off, you darn lion; that's not edible!"

Into the cave, they crawled, one after the other. The group ventured further and further away from the light and warmth; the little cave did get more extensive. They found themselves entering a large, echoed chamber where they could stand. They heard water drip and trickle in the darkness.

"Lilly, it's dark," whispered Squid.

"It's ok, Squid, hold my hand; I got you." Lilly comforted him.

"Apple, is there something you can do about the dark, please?"

"'Please'! From a pirate!? You lot *are* strange … Yeah, maybe- ok, sure, just hold up a sec. Now, lion, stay still while I climb on your back."

"*Squeak … squeak.*" said Tiny as he shook his head.

"Please, Tiny," asked Squid.

"*Squeakily.*"

Apple climbed up Tiny's back, grabbing a big fistful of black-and-white fur as he went.

"*Squeak!*" Tiny protested.

"Keep still, would-ya?" said Apple as he slowly stood up on Tiny's back, his wings fluttering. "That's it. Almost ... almost … gotcha!" Apple clapped his hands together, and something pink glowed between his fingers, illuminating his face.

"What's that?" asked Squid.

"This is a *tinkle puff.*"

Apple shook the tiny creature; a chiming sound filled the cave. Then, all of a sudden, another little creature started to glow off in the darkness. It tooted a high clear note, resounding throughout the cave - then another and another flickered on, all around them: yellows, emeralds, blues, and pinks, twinkling. Slight notes of music poured forth as their glow lit up the cave; the creatures floated then twirled through the air.

"What are they?" asked Squid as he looked around in wonder as he held out his hand, and an electric blue tinkle puff landed on the tip of his finger. He held it close to his face and heard a tiny electric guitar solo strum forth.

"They're tinkle puffs, is what I said."

"Yeah, but what *are* they?"

"Oh, they're seeds of the great singing trees, little lives of every shape and colour ready to sprout and grow."

"They're beautiful … thank you, Apple." Lilly smiled.

"You are very strange for pirates," said Apple, with a bit of rose colouring his green cheeks and a cheeky smile spreading across his face. "Yeah, well, it's not too bad here if you know the trick; Hey, lion, do you mind if I take a load off?"

"*Squeak,*" shrugged Tiny. Apple got comfortable, lounging on Tiny's back as they all meandered on through the cave, surrounded by the music of life flickering all around them. It looked as though three companions had now become four.

Chapter 6 - Boulders & Stones -

"Lilly, I think I see an opening …?" called Squid.

The four companions hurried over, hungry for fresh air and wide-open spaces; popping their heads from the narrow cave, they looked up at the mammoth-sized world around them.

Everything was oversized: mushrooms the size of fat, squishy armchairs, mattress-thick emerald moss, towering feather ferns, and Jurassic-sized singing trees that were so gigantic and so tall that they went up and up, dwarfing everything, even the boulders that lay against them. The leaves of the singing trees were so thick and tightly clustered that they blocked out the sun above. But there were tinkle puffs everywhere, lighting the forest with their soft glow as they lazily swished about on the sighing breeze. Fat crimson moths with translucent ruby wings flipped and flapped their way through the twilight forest, seeking out the dangling pink trumpet flowers, where they unfurled their curly neon tongues and slurped up the golden glowing nectar. Vigorous vines twined around boulders and up the singing trees, covered in clumps of iridescent tiny green leaves and prongs of star-bloomed flowers, which drifted down like falling snow, reflecting the soft twilight as delicate moth wings brushed against them.

"*Squeak.*"

"Wow."

"Cool."

"Yeah … *not bad.*"

Something shot out from the trees above …

SPAAARRCHOOooooshhhhh! A sparkly silver comet with wings powered through the air, arcing around straight towards them.

"Watch out!" warned Lilly.

The comet hit the ground with a little explosion, blowing a puff of moss and grass up into the air, and then churned towards them in a power-slide; a guitar rift ripped out of it: ***Twiddle-deee-DARRRRRRR!***

They all jumped back except Apple, who stood his ground with his hands on his hips, rolling his eyes. The comet came to a screeching stop before him, steam billowing into the air.

"Hello, Daria," Apple sighed.

The steam cleared, unveiling a fairy girl kneeling on the ground, smiling up at them; she had on these old leather pilot goggles, which she pushed to her forehead, revealing shimmering almond-shaped green eyes that twinkled and danced. She flipped her mass of curly lavender hair, which wafted slowly like gravity didn't exist. Leaves and sticks were stuck in there, and the occasional red daisy. Her dress was lovely - woven from tiny silver chains, it sparkled in the soft light - and upon her feet were oversized black leather, silver- buckled stompy boots, which went incredibly well with the snowy white electric guitar that was all angles and points, which she lovingly held to her.

"Hey, Cuz … What's you got there?"

"Nothin', now go away!"

"How is nothin' somethin'? When nothin' is right there behind ya!? Hold up … that's not nothin' … that somethin' is … PIRATES!!! *UuuUUARRRRRRRRRRR!!!*" Daria ran around in circles yelling at the top of her voice, "PIRATES! … HERE! … PIRATES!"

"Daria, *SHHHHHHHHHHH SHHHHHH … shhhh … shh-SHOOSHHH!*" Apple pleaded.

"What?" the fairy said as, looking over her shoulder, she tripped over a rock and fell onto the ground. "OWww … That hurt," she cried, a little tear welling in her eye as she held her knee.

Squid walked over to Daria and offered her a hand up. "It sometimes hurts when you hit your knee, but I do find it's better when someone is there to help you back up," Squid said with a friendly smile.

Daria dried her eyes as she took his hand and smiled a small smile, "Thank you. You are … *very* strange pirates. Hey, Apple! Where- ya find this lot?"

"Well, I was just out an' about in the glen, minding my own business ... when I stumbled on them. They seemed interesting folk, and …"

"*Mindin' your own business!?* Ha! You never minded anything in your whole darn life, Apple! You were doing that pie thing again, weren't you? Last time, you lost part of ya wing to that savage seagull. Look, there's the bite mark! Next time, you gonna lose something important - like ya, head!"

"Ok … ok, I was just havin' a bit of fun, but I did meet these strange pirates, and they're … they're … nice!"

Daria looked over the pirates with a critical eye, then walked around them, looking them up and down and making *HMmmmm hmmMm* noises as she walked. She suddenly grabbed hold of one of Tiny's ears and pulled him down to look inside.

"*SQUEAK!*" squawked Tiny.

"Stay still, you oversized lion," Daria muttered as she peered in … "Hmm, nothin' in there," she said, letting go of Tiny's ear.

"What do you think?" asked Apple, looking a little nervous.

"Well, ok ... They seem perfectly lovely," said Daria, with a big smile and a little twirl of her sparkly dress. "So why did you come through there? If the trollems spot you, you'd be squashed and squelched. *Uugggg*, just thinking about it makes my tummy all squirmy. They like to splash around in your bits … Yuck!"

"What!? … *trollems* … Apple! Did you know about the trollem-thingies?" Lilly asked.

"Kinda … maybe. You see, you're pirates, and it was like, yeah … But I didn't know that you were … nice before ... Which, by the way, is ***odd!*** Then we were just going this way, and I kinda forgot about the trollems, and then we were talking and having a great time and …"

"You were leading us into a trap?"

"Yeah … Sorry."

"Are they around?" asked Lilly in a hushed voice as she peered around.

"Yep!" Daria piped up.

"Where?"

Daria pointed around to some exceptionally large, curious-looking boulders lying against the singing trees and further off in the forest. "There … there ... Oh, and over there."

"But they're just rocks … ?" questioned Squid.

Daria flew up to Squid, hovering over his shoulder. "Look," she said, pointing slowly from one spot to another.

Squid spoke, "Hey, that biggish stone - it looks like a big toe! I mean 'toes'… if you follow that bit back. That's a lumpish belly. Oh, Lilly, they're all around."

Lilly and Tiny looked about the forest; they started to realise that the boulders and stones weren't boulders and stones at all but huge round bellies, big knobbly knees, massive feet and fat, long fingers poking up through the moss and shrubbery. The trollems were sprawled about the Jurassic-sized forest, sleeping soundly, hardly moving. Their chests gently rose and fell with each long breath; the sighing of the wind that blew through the forest was not a breeze after all; it was the breath from the great lungs of the trollems that whirled and twirled the tinkle puffs around.

Flowers and shrubbery grew on the stony figures forming part of their clothes, which helped to keep them so well hidden. One of the trollems had a great knobbly head, resembling a gigantic white potato with closed sunken eyes. Scraggly roots grew from its face, and its clothes were made from living green ivy weaved into overalls. White mushrooms sprouted out between its fat bulbous toes. A dark and lovely-looking immense trollem lady was sound asleep, curled against a fallen tree. She had tiny pink flowers splashed across her cheeks, they looked just like little freckles, and her hair was an afro of purple flowers. White blossoms bloomed all down her dark-green moss dress. The last trollem that they could see was just immense and muscular. He was lying on his side; his great, dark, broad back was turned towards them. His skin was speckled-polished, black stone.

"So, Apple, why are you feeding these guys to the trollems?"

"I'm not … anymore!"

"Yeah … they're kinda nice for pirates."

At that moment, Squid's tummy rumbled. Then Tiny's tummy rumbled.

"*SHHHHHHHHHHHH!!!*" they all said, except for Daria.

"Oh, you're going to Kitchen's - that's why you're going this way!"

"URRRrrrrrr …"

"What was that?" Squid asked.

They all slowly turned; the trollem closest to them, with the potato head, was moving! They stared frozen to the spot, as the trollem's mouth opened wide with a cavernous bone-cracking yawn:

"UURRROOoOOGGGHHH!"

Fat orange bugs scurried about its corn-yellow peg-like teeth; the trollem chomped down its big gob, crushing and chewing the bugs to a chunky blue goo, which gushed down its root-covered chin. The trollem slowly rolled towards them, tearing up moss and ferns as its big fungus-coated hand tore free of the undergrowth and swept out and over them, forcing them all to duck. The giant limb passed slowly over, raining down debris. Then trollem's hand sprawled in the moss behind them with a ***THUD!*** Blocking the small cave opening, its other hand slapped its face, scratching as it smiled in satisfaction and went back to sleep.

Apple whispered, "Well, no going back now; we'll just have to fly over and down to Kitchen's."

"Fly?" whispered Squid.

"Yes. Fly."

"Um, Apple …?

"Yes, Squid?"

"We don't have any wings."

"Oh … I forgot that bit. Well, we … Ok … maybe … we'll …. Yeah… sure. That's it! Catapult!"

"Catapult?" asked Lilly.

"*Squeak* … *Squeak* …" squeaked Tiny.

"Cata ... catapol … catapult?" asked Squid.

"See these big ferns? They're not any old ferns; they're bus-vaulting rubbertastic ferns. Here, if you grab one at the top like this, pull it down, and wrap it around your waist until you can't turn anymore. Ok, got it; then you lift your feet, so it takes your weight, and just touch the ground with your toe …"

TWAAANNNGGGGGG!

"*ITT'Ss …*"

"*Thaatt …*"

"*EEEEEEEAAASSSYYY!*"

Apple shot up, through the air, up … up … up he went, arms, legs, and wings all a-tumble, disappearing out of sight.

Daria looked at the others.

"Well, that looks like fun and all, but … *bye!*" With that, she blasted off with a loud ***BANG!*** Silver sparkles rained down as she zipped off, up through the leafy branches.

"AUUUURRR … What was … that … noise?"

The trollems started moving, climbing to their feet, and rubbing their eyes. Gargantuan singing trees shook, metallic leaves tinkled from above, and rubbertastic ferns stretched and twanged about. Crimson moths fled with big flippy flaps of their wings as tinkle puffs swirled through the air.

"Who? WHAT? Woke us up?"

The potato trollem stretched as he spoke, cracking his back and then his thick neck, which crackled like bunches of branches snapping, as he towered above them. Then, lastly, the lady trollem rolled to her side and spoke:

“Oh, I was having such a lovely dream and all. There was pirate chunky jelly, pirate soufflé, and Vegemite pirate. Oh my! I do love a Vegemite pirate.”

Lilly whispered to the group. “Go, everyone, go!”

“Oi, Petal, is that a dream or real?”

The lady trollem pointed at the group. Squid couldn’t *go* - he had just stopped ... Lilly glanced over at her little brother. He wasn’t moving. Squid was just standing there looking at the mossy ground. She stepped close to him and went to put her arm around him but saw Squid’s shoulders tense, and his hands began to shake; he hadn’t been like this in ages.

“Augie, you got this,” she said, standing near her brother but not touching him.

“*Squeak?*” Tiny came up and also stood close to Squid and then held out his paw.

Squid reached out and smoothed the fur on Tiny’s arm, and then he slowly turned and looked up to Lilly.

“Yeah, I got this.” He walked, then ran and jumped, grabbing the tip of a bus-vaulting rubbertastic fern, spinning as he did, wrapping the fern about his waist. The fern slowly bent down till his toes touched against the ground; then he turned and smiled, and *BOOOOINNNNGG!* He flipped through the air up, and up he went, yelling, "Whooo-HOOOOOOO!"

The stone trollem started sniffing, huffing the air.

ARHF-nNIFF, ARHF-nNIFF

"I smell …" - *nnNIFF* - "PIRATE! I see pirate … That be reeeeaaal, Nancy."

"Oh really!?"

She clapped her extensive hands with a loud ***CRACK!*** as she stood up, knocking stray plants and dirt from her moss dress.

"We can have Vegemite pirate. Yeah!"

She smiled a big, big smile and did a little jump as she giggled; the ground trembled as her moss-dress twirled, and her purple- bloomed hair swayed back and forth gaily.

"I do love fresh pirate for brekkie. When you toast 'em and butter 'em up and smear 'em all over with yummy-tummy Vegemite … They're crunchy and tangy on the outside and soft and chewy in the middle. It's incredible!"

Lilly pushed Tiny, hissing, "Go, Tiny, go!" as she looked up at the towering trollems.

"*SQUEEEK,*" squeaked Tiny as he ran.

"Look! It's a little furry one - they tickle when you chomp'em down … *Hee, hee, heee.*"

The tremendous dark polished-head trollem spoke; his voice sounded like a bucket of grinding gravel as he stomped towards Tiny. Tiny ran as fast as his furry legs could; he leapt, grabbing a fern tip in his teeth. His body spun round and round, wrapping the rubbertastic fern around him from nose to tail. The fern bent with his weight. Tiny touched one furry toe to the ground, and … *BOOOOINNNNGG!* The massive trollem tried to catch him - his chunky hands swept up, but Tiny sailed straight through.

"*SQUEEEEEEEEEEEKKKK!*" he squeaked, disappearing through the treetops.

"OI! Come back down. Why so high?"

The bald trollem grumbled. Lilly watched as the stone beast turned and started stomping towards her, singing trees swaying and shaking around them. Massive arms and legs swung, squishing plants, bus-vaulting rubbertastic ferns bent and twanged as the trollems came for her.

"I want jelly between my wiggles!"

The lady trollem cried out as they pushed and shoved at each other in their hurry.

Lilly ran through the forest dodging behind singing trees. The trollems gave chase, their massive feet pounding the ground, but their legs were so long they caught up to her quickly; they surrounded her. Lilly looked up at their hungry, grinning faces as they huffed, puffed and leered down at her. They sang:

"STOMPY, STOMPY, SQUISHING TIME!"

Then:

Bang, BOOM! Bang!

Hands and feet rained down on Lilly; she ducked, dodged, ran, and jumped as vast fists came down from above, and great feet stomped and kicked, but she was too quick for them.

"Hold still!"

But she would not - around legs, over feet, she jumped.

"Quit jumpin'!"

The ground bounced and shook, but she ran, weaving in and out.

"OWWWW! That's not pirate; THAT ME FOOT! … SHUV OFF!"

BOOOOOM!

The trollems started whacking each other, with great slaps of hands against stony flesh, the crunching and smacking sound ringing throughout the forest. Lilly dived between the legs of a trollem.

CRASHHHH!

One of the trollems was knocked to the ground before her; it bounced and jiggled to a stop. Lilly jumped high onto its potato face, squishing its nose and lips with her boots.

"OWWrr! Nott mee ppetty faceth!"

The potato trollem protested through squished lips. Lilly leapt high off its face and came down with both feet nice and straight onto its big, rounded belly. The belly squished down deep, and in she went. Down … down … a great whoosh of air wheezed out of the trollem's lungs as she sunk.

HHORRSHHHSHHH …

Suddenly the trollem gasped in a voluminous trollem breath.

wwWHHAAHUUA!

Its sunken belly **inflated!** Exploding Lilly out at tremendous speed and up like she was being shot from a cannon. Up through the branches of the singing trees, up through their thick leaves, up into the bright blue sky above, shooting far away from the trollems as they called,

"COME BACK, JELLY!"

And the lady trollem said sadly,

"What about my Vegemite pirate!?"

While the speckled stone trollem ground out,

"OI, YOU COULD HAVE STAYED FOR A BITE OR THREEEE!"

Over the treetops, Lilly sailed, the wind whistling by. Daria flew up alongside her. "Lilly, I didn't know you could fly! How wonderful!" The fairy exclaimed with an enormous grin.

"I can't!" said Lilly worriedly.

"Oh, … how dreadful … Well, then … tootles!" said Daria happily as she flew off, leaving Lilly to her descent.

"DARIA!!" Lilly yelled as she continued falling through the trees smashing through the scratchy branches; she tried to grab onto something, but the branches snapped; nothing would stop her fall. Panicked, Lilly lashed out for anything to hold onto, but still, she fell.

Chapter 7 – Kitchen -

… THURRRLLOP!

Lilly was stuck up to her neck in some kinda clear-orange-jelly mushroom thingy; her arms couldn't move; her legs couldn't move - she just, sort of, wobbled about; she tried to pull her arms or legs free but could only manage to wibble and wobble about some more.

"Hey, Sis,"

Lilly turned her head, and her little brother sat on a lime-green toadstool shaped like a puffy sun chair. He was eating a slice of pavlova! It had cream, strawberries, bananas, and chocolate sprinkles.

"That looks good, Squid. Could you give me a hand?"

"*MMMM,* yep, in a sec - this is good."

"*Augie.*"

"Ok, ok … KITCHEN!" he called. Something crashed towards them.

Thump … thump …

Thump … thump …

Something humungous peered around a Jurassic-sized singing tree.

"TROLLEM!" Lilly screamed … "RUN, SQUID … RUN!" Lilly frantically tried again to pull herself out of her sticky situation, but she only wibbled about, the same as before. Squid just smiled and took another bite of his pavlova.

Thump … thump …

Thump … thump …

A substantial, warm brown hand reached down towards her with immaculate, manicured nails. Lilly screamed, "AHHHHHHHHH!" up at a singular, massive-lovely smiling face. The trollem picked her and the orange mushroom up all in one hand and gave her a good shake. Her head whipped back and forth as orange goo sloshed off her. Orange jelly mushrooms sprouted up wherever the goo landed, jiggling, and grew till they were the size of the one Lilly had just floundered in. The trollem put her down gently and gave her a little pat on the head, knocking her captain's hat down over her eyes. Lilly popped her hat back up as the trollem turned and sauntered off.

Thump … thump …

Thump … thump …

Squid quickly munched down the rest of his sugary meringue slice and ran over to Lilly, grabbing her hand. "You ok, Sis?" he asked, looking up at her. Lilly stood there, feeling a little freaked out as she watched the trollem stomp out of sight.

"Squid, did that trollem have an apron on, with little daises!?"

"Oh, that's just Kitchen. Yeah, she liked my bandana. Come on." Squid tugged and pulled, dragging Lilly along the path through the tinkle-puff-lighted forest. Singing trees towered above them, jelly mushrooms wibbled, and bus-vaulting rubbertastic ferns swayed and twanged in the twilight.

Lilly could hear something. "Squid, what's that sound?"

"It's just around the corner; come on," Squid replied as he jogged off. Lilly followed him, the forest opening to a blue sky and a great bend of a wide river, which … steamed?! The water was hot, the steam twirling and swirling above it. Squid watched the water with a bit of a smile on his face. Lilly walked down to the rocky edge and looked out over the water. She could just see a large flat rock sticking out in the river, a long jump away.

"Hey, Sis, watch this!" Before Lilly could do anything, Squid had run past her and then jumped, soaring through the air and landing on the flat rock in the river; he then jumped again! and disappeared into the steaming mist. "Come on, Lilly!" he called back.

"CRIKEY! Squid, where are you going?" Lilly yelled out to him, but he didn't answer. She would have to go after the little squirt. Lilly backed up, then backed up some more. Then she sprinted hard and fast and jumped, windmilling her arms. Through the air, she soared, landing out on the flat rock. Lilly looked out into the twirling mist. There was another flat rock ahead; *she thought they must be set out as big steppingstones; this must be how the trollem had come.*

She ran and jumped after that numskull of a brother, stone to stone. First, she was scared and worried that she would fall, but her worries soon faded, and she was flying. She laughed as the mist whipped by, jump, jump, jump, and jump! She flew.

Then a monumental door loomed out of the thick mist, and she smacked full speed into it. "OW! Bloomin', really!" she complained, rubbing at her shoulder.

Lilly took a step back, then another and another as she looked up and up. The door was really, stupendously big - the size of a two- storey house - and was mounted into the dark stone of the cliff face. It was made from polished ebony timbers but had all these doors of different shapes and sizes stuck into it, from top to bottom; they were all over the place. Each was brightly painted, and some tiny doors had little porches sticking out. There were round doors, barn doors, grand doors, arched doors, hatches, and cat flaps. There were porcelain bells that jingled, ropes that you pulled, big copper knockers for knocking, and even little silvered bells that tinkled. *They must be there to announce themselves,* she thought. And there, high above her head, on the right-hand side, was a mighty-sized cast- iron doorknob inlaid with golden letters saying: "'WELCOME.'"

"*Hmmm,*" she murmured.

A whirring sound filled the air behind her. She turned and looked. Fairies flew out of the mist; some even looked just like people but with wings: fat ones, green ones, thin ones, dark ones, tall ones, purple ones, tiny ones - all came tumbling towardsthe doors. Coloured mohawks, big round fuzzy hair, glowing, glittering rhinestones, thick chunky leather belts, flared trousers, chains of silver, suits of armour, straw hats, and Hawaiian shirts; and mixed in with them all was a swarm of small blue creatures with Elvis's hair.

The air was filled with strange, weird, and just … beatifically awesome people! Each would fly to a door and politely knock or chime a bell or pound a knocker. Silver bells jingled, horns honked, knockers knocked, and chimes tingled, filling the air with a musical noise. Then their doors would open, and through they went, *Squid, Tiny, and Apple must be behind these doors somewhere,* she thought. So, Lilly stood back and looked about for a door for herself, but nothing seemed to take her fancy.

Then a twinkle caught her eye between a cottage door and a bejewelled cat flap; it sparkled at her. She walked over and peered closer and closer, kneeling on one knee for a better look. It was a tiny little door, the size of the end of her finger; it was simply perfect and so lovely that she reached out and touched it - and it bit her.

"OW! What? FLOOMIN' CRIKEY!" she cried, sticking her swollen finger into her mouth and sucking on it to stop the bleeding. Lilly glared at the itty-bitty door. "You, rotten little thing," she said. The teensy door shined red for a second and started to grow, pushing and shoving the other entries out of the way. The other doors grumbled and complained as it grew, shifted, and shoved, getting bigger and bigger until the door had grown to just the right size for her; her very own, made from driftwood, with a single porthole window. Fairies flooded past her through their doors. Lilly thought she better knock to be polite, as all the other fairies had to ***knock*** … ***knock, knock*** … She struck with the scrolled brass knocker against the wood. The door clicked and swung open. Righting her hat, she stepped on through.

A fairy flashed in front of her … wearing some uniform. She was smallish, only coming up to around Lilly's waist. The fairy wore rather large diamond-faceted-crystal glasses, which made it look like she had lots and lots of deep coffee-coloured eyes, which swivelled in different directions, constantly moving, looking up and around at all the entrance ways. Her long curly, springy chocolate-caramel hair floated and wafted, bouncing around her. The fairy held a relatively thick golden notepad and a quill from a long black cockatoo feather. She sort-of blurred and shimmered in and out of focus as Lilly looked at her. Lilly realised that the same fairy standing in front of her was multiplied and with all the other creatures, peoples, and things simultaneously as with her. So, just as each fairy came through their doors, this same fairy would materialize in front of them. Lilly looked back to the fairy in front of her, who was shifting in and out of focus as her assorted eyes scanned the doors for customers; Lilly noticed the fairy was only solid for perhaps half a second while she spoke.

"ORDER," she said.

"What?" asked Lilly. The fairy's coffee-coloured eyes focused on her all at once and blinked.

"ORDER!" the fairy repeated, her wings a blurring buzz at her back as her beautiful springy hair undulated around her.

"'Order' what?'" asked Lilly.

"Order anything!" the fairy replied in exasperation as her eyes wandered off, looking in different directions, and she blurred in and out of focus once more.

"Anything?"

"Yes, anything!" said the fairy.

At that moment, the smell hit Lilly's nostrils: chocolate chip cookies, lasagne, strawberry ice cream, pumpkin soup, fish and chips, honey prawns, tikka masala, sweet potato pie, BBQ pork, custard, fried chicken, and pizza. It smelt so … yum! The more she sniffed, the more she smelled. The spices and the aromas were incredible! Lilly's mouth watered.

"ORDER!'" said the fairy.

"Trifle," Lilly uttered without a thought. It was her favourite at Christmas time. The fairy quickly scratched it down on her notepad, her long black feathered quill whipping back and forth.

"Name?"

"Lilly – oh, I mean Captain Red Lilly."

"Reservation for Captain Red Lilly: Level 12, Table 9, Seat 4." She added that to the order slip, promptly tore it off, and threw it into the air; off it went of its own accord down through the hallway, disappearing out of sight. "Move on, move on, make way … Whoops! You nearly made me forget. Hold a moment; we can't have you just going anywhere!" The fairy spun a strange machine from around her back. It was silvered, with buttons and twirly bits, and it had a big red lever on its left-hand side.

The fairy punched some buttons and twisted some knobbly things. The machine jittered, twirled, and swirled; the fairy pulled the red lever, and the machine blasted - ***BING!*** And out popped a ticket stub with a *PSST* of sparkly strawberry-smelly smoke, which quickly dispersed into the air stirred by the fairy's buzzing wings; the fairy handed over the ticket stub.

"There we go, all set. Welcome to Kitchen's, Kia-ora … Now, Move ON! MOVE ON!"

Lilly walked away from the monumental, strange door and the irritable buzzing fairy. The walkway was carpeted with twinkly soft moss that shimmered as she stepped. Flying fairies passed overhead through clouds of winking purple, silver, and blue twinkle puffs; all of them headed in the same direction, deeper into the mountain.

Lilly was underground, inside an enormous rock corridor. The walls were covered with iridescent, coloured fungi and mushrooms, which looked like beautiful coral from the Great Barrier Reef. Shimmering glow bugs darted in and out around the glowing fungus, just like schools of fish - swishing one way, then flashing another.

She walked along till she came to an ornate red stone balcony overlooking a tremendous auditorium. It must have once been part of the natural cavern system but had been enlarged and shaped. Scrolled carved stone columns ran up the walls to the domed ceiling high above, supporting balcony after balcony, landings, and nooks, one after another, going up and up, floor after floor, creating a spectacular view of the orchestrated chaos in the magnificent kitchen far below. There was the trollem who had helped her out of the jelly mushroom!

The trollem was now wearing a tall white chef's hat but still had on her apron with the daises. Standing in the middle of the most fantastic kitchen, she was spinning, flipping, whisking, baking, poaching, and sautéing; a beatific smile of pure happiness and joy lit up her face as she looked up to the large crowds above. Fairy chefs dodged in and out all around her. They wore puffy slouching hats and white chef outfits, carrying dishes or ingredients, cooking, and creating. Saucepans and cauldrons bubbled and spat on fiery trollem sized stoves. Huge flames flared and rolled up into the auditorium air as the trollem chef danced and flambéed.

Off to the side, just above the kitchen, the golden order slips swarmed: a twirling shimmering mass surrounding a very fat fairy with a mammoth moustache and tiny wings wearing the same type of maroon uniform as the fairy at the door; he dangled in the air, held up by a flinging bus-vaulting rubbertastic fern, bouncing and zipping and swaying through the auditorium, snatching golden order slips as he the fern flung him through the swirling mass. He yelled the orders out, loud and clear, to the kitchen below, sounding a lot like one of those speedy auctioneers from Texas. Now and then, he would take a great gasping breath between orders. “L-7, T-10, S-6: gilded-fungus, béarnaise-sauce! L-3, T-7, S-1: sausage-sanger! L- 10, T-1, S-2: snoodle-wellington! “*HuuuuUAH!*” he gasped, then away he went again. “L-3, T-1, S-2: chilli glow-bug kebabs!”

When they were ready, dishes shot up into the air, flung or thrown from the kitchen below. Servers dive-bombed down from above, catching the meals and whisking them up and away without spilling a thing; it was pretty spectacular.

Lilly leaned out over the balcony and looked up. Warm, soft light filtered down from above from a prodigious, odd bulbous chandelier, which hung, mounted to the centre of the tremendous domed stone ceiling; from the chandelier dangled down long lines of blue pulsating lights, which slowly swished back and forth through the air, surrounded by swirling shimmering glow bugs. The whole place was strange: glowing fungus grew upon the walls and dotted the ceilings, filling the underground with soft candlelight. Fairies of all shapes and sizes drank and ate in all the galleries and alcoves. Some clinked stone mugs together, sloshing golden bubbling foam while others sipped from dainty curly glasses which streamed purple smoke as gritty laughter boomed and piping happy silliness echoed, the chatter of a thousand fairies.

Lilly took in the spectacle when a tall, well-muscled curly blond-haired fairy approached her. She wore a little black bow tie and the same maroon suit that seemed to be the standard attire in Kitchen’s kitchen.

“Table number, please,” the female fairy grumbled. Lilly handed over her ticket stub. “*HMMMmmm,*” the fairy said, taking out a pair of petite glasses, which she held up with just two fingers holding them close to her eyes. The fairy read Lilly's ticket aloud, barking, "Level 12, Table 9, Seat 4," as she pointed across and up. "Wings?" she questioned, putting her glasses away into a small pocket.

"No, but where are the stairs or a lift?" asked Lilly.

The fairy gave her a purse-lipped look as she unclasped a curled horn from her belt and placed it against her lips, trumpeting out from the balcony, "LEVEL 12, TABLE 9, SEAT 4, NO WINGS!"

Lilly looked around. There were no stairs and no way to get down or up? … There was just the way back?

The fairy turned to Lilly as she attached her horn back to her.

"Ready?" the fairy said.

"Ready for what exactly?"

At this, the fairy suddenly grabbed Lilly, one hand at the back of her shirt, scrunching it up, and the other gripping her belt. "OI! Unhand me, you big oaf! I am Captain Red Lilly of the ship *Ches* ..." The fairy lifted her into the air, jiggling her about, judging her weight, jolting her up and down, and then the fairy started spinning. The world flickered around, and around Lilly got dizzier and dizzier. "PUT … MEEE … DOWNNNNNN! …" she demanded, and casually the fairy let go. Over the railing, out into the open air, she went, falling and tumbling Lilly, let out a yell, "ARGHHHHHH, BLOOMIN NOT AGAAAIN!" and plummeted straight down towards the kitchen, with its rolling flames and boiling pots. Servers flew past her with trays of food and drinks and odd bubbling cauldron's trailing bubbles, pulsating with twisting emerald flames, down, past level, after level, she fell; Lilly held her captain's hat against her head with both hands and squinted her eyes, and, and …

Yoink! She stopped short. Lilly now dangled, saved from certain death, high in the air. Something had a hold of one of her boots. She looked slowly up: it was a pint-sized, maroon-suited fairy, his little wings buzzing madly. The fairy spoke in a high, nasally voice. “Welcome to Kitchens ‘Miss-and-clean service’. Or, as luck has it today, ‘Catch-and-lift service.’ Level 12, Table 9, Seat 4, this way, please,” and up they went.

“Thanks?!” she called up to her carrier, hoping her luck would hold till she got to wherever she was going.

Up and up, they flew, level after level; finally, the little fairy flew her over to an extensive chiselled-out gallery filled with strange, odd diners.

“Lilly, you’re here; what took you so long?” asked Squid.

“*Squeak?*” squeaked Tiny.

“Lilly, grab a seat,” said Apple.

The fairy waiter plonked her down - *OOMPH!* - on top of a grey mushroom-chair, face down, legs and arms all tangled.

“Level 12, Table 9, Seat 4. Drink waiter will be here shortly,” he chirped as he left.

Exasperated, Lilly righted herself and looked around. Squid, Apple, and Tiny had big goofy smiles on their faces. Other tables were scattered around them, some placed into smaller alcoves carved into the stone walls. Some fairies were teeny, and some were people-sized, eating spectacular dishes: levitating doughnuts, upside-down cake, which was plated on the ceiling, with matching upside-down diners; steaming soup, in which slippery black things swam, and immense bright red clawed cockroaches drenched in rich garlic-butter sauce, glowing jelly bulbs filled with fizzy drinks, that made their drinkers speak in burps, whilst the bitsy fairies were blown backwards by their explosive belches.

Two skinny people-sized things … darkly cloaked and hooded, were sitting at a table for two, off in a small, shadowed alcove. A glint of silver shone where their eyes should have been. Their long- clawed hands moved expressively over a glowing smouldering bowl covered in inscriptions. The two creatures tilted back their heads; the coloured smoke streamed up to their sucking mouths hidden by their shadowed hoods.

Another table had a large silver platter with some type of roasted creature, seven crooked legs, and fat rounded toes poked up into the air. Seven farmer fairies sat around the roasted animal, looking rather happy and hungry. Their waiter lit the dish with a snap of his fingers: a spark flashed, and a whoosh of blue-and-green flames sizzled the beast with pops and crackles. A lovely aroma filled the air. The seven fairies gasped in delight and clapped their hands, each tearing off succulent, juicy, rounded legs as the blue and green flames ebbed and died. Everyone seemed to be having a pretty good time in all.

"How was your flight? … Fun, huh?" said Squid with a smile.

"More like 'terrifying,'" Lilly replied as she looked around their table, wondering what it was; It was a mushroom, pink and grey on top and yellow underneath, with matching chairs. The chairs were soft and comfortable. Glowing fungus dotted the ceiling in living mounds, giving off a warm yellow soft light,adding to the cosy atmosphere. A fairy waiter fluttered up to their alcove, balancing a drink tray.

"Watermelon with a twist of spearmint for Seat 3."

"*Squeak,*" squeaked Tiny.

"Triple chocolate super-thick-thick-shake with chocolate sprinkles and whipped vanilla cream for Seat 2."

"Thanks," Squid said.

"Rhubarb and celery iced tea with extra olives and extra dirty, shaken, not stirred, Seat 1."

"Kia-ora," replied Apple.

"And what can I do for you?" the waiter addressed Lilly. Lilly looked up at the fairy, their eyes locked; everything grew distant for a second. "Wonderful, back in a jiffy." With that, he dove off the balcony edge.

"But I didn't order," Lilly said.

"Yeah, you did," said Apple. "You just didn't use any words." He wiggled his fingers in her direction. "*They read your mind.*"

"Don't worry, Lilly, it's great," Squid said as he tried to slurp away on his super-thick-thick-shake, his cheeks sucked in.

"So, what happened to you guys after the trollems?" asked Lilly.

Squid wiped some vanilla cream off his face.

"Well, we were stuck there for a bit, then Kitchen turned up, and there was some screaming and yelling, then she gave me some pavlova and showed us the way here, and then I went back and waited for you - and that's about it."

The waiter returned, wings buzzing, "Captain, your drink: nutmeg-spiced hot chocolate topped with roasted pink marshmallows and a swirl of salted caramel."

"Wow! … Thank you, it's just what ... I wanted!" Lilly exclaimed; She took a sip. It was simply fabulous. "Apple, what is this place?"

"This is Kitchen's place, and that's Kitchen down there - the big lady."

"Isn't she a trollem, who likes squishing pirates and eating'-em!?"

"'Was' more like it; she gave that up long ago. She couldn't stop cooking - the happier she got, the more she cooked. So, she built this place and started feeding us, it was only a few at first, but more and more came from all over, then she and we just kept on building level after level to fit us all in till it got to, well, this! You see, she's just so happy bringing joy to us and my hungry belly," he added with a smile and a little *burrrp!* The waiter returned, carrying four plates stacked with glorious food. His wings buzzed as he hovered above the table and laid out the dishes.

"Seat 4, trifle."

"Thank you," Lilly said, astounded as she gazed at the layer upon layer of chunky, sugared, orange-soaked biscuits, the chilled thickened vanilla cream, red and orange jelly cubes, and vanilla custard. It teetered and tottered back and forth in the large sapphire crystal bowl, a glazed red cherry perched on the very top. She grabbed a crystal spoon: White chocolate mascarpone, raspberry, juicy orange jellies, silky custard. The flavour was just simply … scrumptious. "Oh, my!" she mumbled as she dug in.

"Seat 2, bangers and mash."

"OH! Yeah," Squid said. A great pile of pillowy white buttery mash potatoes with six chunky pork sausages were stuck all over the place with big dollops of thick brown glossy onion gravy.

"Seat 3, sautéed asparagus with burnt butter white-wine reduction and chilli-honeyed carrots upon roasted wedges of caramelised, salted spring pumpkin."

"*Squeakily, Squeak,*" squeaked Tiny.

"Seat 1, the cheeseburger tower, with extra gherkins and a side of double-length French fries with blue-bug hot sauce and morning-mouse mayo."

"Yeah, baby, yeah!" exclaimed Apple.

Across the way, on the other side of the auditorium, the fungus grew brighter in a domed chiselled-out gallery, illuminating a jazz band below; white-suited fairies of all colours, shapes, and sizes stood on fungus platforms. They had trumpets, a piano, drums, saxophone, and electric guitars. The jazz band started playing a catchy, jazzy tune, which rolled out and around the auditorium as they danced to the beat.

A tall fairy with deep russet-brown skin strolled out from amid the band with a funky walk, snapping his fingers. He wore a bright yellow zoot suit, an oversized black bow tie, and a wide-brimmed yellow hat; his purple-thumping butterfly wings shimmered and flipped to the beat. He started a crazy whirling dance, then strutted forward, his knees wobbling back and forth in time with the music. He strode out onto a purplish mushroom that jutted out into the air of the auditorium. There he stood, smiling with oversized, perfect white teeth. He looked around at the audience, his back to the band, polishing his knuckles on his jacket intently. The crowd started clapping and cheering but soon grew silent as the fairy looked up from under his oversized yellow hat, and then he began to sing.

"A boy wandered far, where it was wild - a guitar his weapon, his voice a hurricane of fire.

"He sought the Fae Queen, who haunted his every hour.

"On stone doors, he stumbled. Far, in lands seldom trod by man.

"No lock, no handle?

"Silent he stopped and stood. His guitar flickered to his hand, which trickled then streamed, then roared. His voice rose and broke to a storm. Stone doors blazed, rippled, and raged. The veil was torn.

"Fae creatures rustled and began to wail and swirled in through that torn veil.

"Queen of Fae quickened with that untethered sound and saw that the boy was uncrowned."

"She sang. Be mine, you're mine, your soul is mine, so join the line, all stomp in time. I'm the party, so join the party, oh mortal mine.

"All that heard were beholden when her mouth did open. The weird and wonderful came from all around to see the queen, which all are bound.

Fairies fluttered from their tables and alcoves, dancing, laughing, spinning, and summersaulting through the air, holding their partners tight, feet flying to the jazzy music; they enjoyed themselves without a care. Wings twinkled and shimmered in the reflected glow of the fungus chandelier. Tinkle puffs swirled, glittering on the wing-stirred breeze, all twirling about in the open air.

"She is thorn, she is flower.

"She draws all, from all around, to party under that mound. The boy did sing; he lost his heart to the fairy queen who was hot.

"Oh boy, his guitar did wail to the mighty queen who we all hail!

"His voice broke, his guitar sighed, his gaze lingered ... Behind stone doors, he wandered, to dance beside a queen he wanted.

To rock delights of immortal rights, to please a queen, all right ...

"She has a taste for mortal lives, The boy survived with immortal pride, but no one gets out alive. As hell was his treasure, stone doors locked forever.

"She's the party, so rock that party.

"And hail the mistress of time, for now, and forever, Oh queen of satisfied!"

Kitchen's kitchen erupted in applause as the patrons clapped and whistled in admiration for the band.

"Is it like, this all the time?" Lilly called above the noise as she also clapped and cheered.

"This place is brilliant!" said Squid, banging his knife and fork on the mushroom table and stomping his feet, echoing others around him.

"Well, yeah, this is about an average day for Kitchen's kitchen. The Fae come from all over, doing business, visiting family, or sightseeing. Then you've got your Festival ofthe Under-song, which is … EPIC!"

"*Under-song* - what's that?" asked Squid.

"It's what connects us and all things - and with *her*." As he spoke, the fairies around them looked sharply over at their table, giving Apple a pointed look and a decisive shake of their heads. Apple stopped talking. Then he smiled and said, "Just another blowout in my town. You're welcome anytime; just send a letter first so I can get you around the trollems a little bit easier next time. So, where do you guys call home?" Asked Apple. The fairies around them returned to their chatter and lovely, if not strange, meals.

"*HOME?*" Lilly stood straight up " … MUM! Oh gosh … She is going to kill me! The house, the Tasman Sea, it's in the lounge room! We gotta get home, Squid, like yesterday."

"How? We're out here somewhere, on a bloomin' walkabout: we've got no map, and we got sneezed here by a gimassive fish!"

"*Squeak.*"

"Chester! That's right, Tiny - He will know the way home. Apple, we've got to get back to our ship."

"Ok, keep your britches on," he said as he dipped his finger into his drink and made a little map on the mushroom tabletop. "We're about *here,* inside this mountain; your ship isn't that far. I saw you- lot, skipping across the ocean and ramming up on Short Beach just below the bluff. That's where that darn psychotic Seagull lives - probably still chewing part of my wing," Apple added, grinding his teeth. "See, this island is volcanic, filled with old lava tubes; that's why the river out front is all hot and steamy; it's all from the magma underneath; even Kitchen's kitchen is heated by Vulcan herself."

"'Vulcan'?" Squid asked.

"Yeah, the god of all things hot and smouldery. Now and then, she has a bit of a hissy fit and blows her top - then, this place *really* rocks-and-rolls, if you get my meaning. Anyway, back to the tunnels: below Kitchen's kitchen, there's a big lake with a dock. That's where I'm fairly sure there's a shortcut, which would pop us out near your beach … near my nemesis!"

"Nema … nemesis?" Squid repeated.

"Enemy, scourge, scoundrel, rival, adversary that seagull took part of my wing! I *will* have my revenge."

“Apple, you were a *pie* at the time. Weren’t you?” Lilly pointed out.

“Oh yeah, I forgot that bit.”

“All right. It sounds like a plan; let’s do it. You guys all finished?”

“Hold up, let me have this last mouthful,” said Squid.

“I can’t believe you ate all that.”

“It’s yum - nearly as good as Mum’s,” he replied.

“*Squeak!*” squeaked Tiny.

“Let’s go. Um … Apple? *How* do we go?!” asked Lilly with a bit of apprehension.

“Come to the rail; this won’t take a sec.”

They all groaned as they tried to get up, their bellies all very full. Squid sucked up the last of his super thick-thick shake and let out quite a large *BUUUURRRRROP!* “Excuse me,” he said, smiling and covering his mouth.

“That’s alright, Squid; we all feel the same way.” Lilly got up and walked over to the rail overlooking the kitchen - it was a long way down.

“Waiter, waiter!” Apple called.

“Yes?” The waiter fairy from earlier popped down into view.

“Three for Kitchen’s level, to pay their respects to the chef, no wings.”

“Very well. A moment please … Henry!” the waiter called. A very muscular-looking fairy flew down from above.

“Three for Kitchen level, no wings.”

“Yes, Mr. Gibbons.” Henry’s hands shot out and grabbed Squid by his collar and Tiny by the scruff of his neck, and he tossed them! Over the railing and down, they fell. Lilly screamed, “SQUID! TINY! as she looked over the rail. Apple buzzed over and landed on the rail’s edge, saying, “See ya,” took a single step off and was gone. Lilly turned. Henry just smiled and grabbed her and then threw her, too. Down she plummeted, past dancing fairies, past waiters carrying food and drinks, past a trollem about to be tossed by a bunch of large, straining waitpeople. The trollem looked as worried as Lilly was. She fell through clouds of twinkle puffs, which actually went ***puff!*** When you fell through them. Her eyes watering in the rushing wind, the great flames from Kitchen’s kitchen rolled up and were about to engulf her when ***OOMPF!*** She was caught, and all the air was knocked from her lungs.

“Thaaanks …” she gasped.

“Kitchen level! Thank you for using Kitchen’s ‘Miss and Clean service’ or ‘Catch and Lift service.’ And for surviving our services twice in one day, please accept this coupon for a free fungus jelly of your choice, redeemable on your next survival!” the waiter who caught her chirped as he dropped her on the kitchen landing. Squid and Tiny lay there panting; Apple fluttered down and landed beside them.

Lilly looked up and up to where she had been thrown and said, “I don’t think I could ever get used to that.”

“They only miss once in a while,” Apple said.

"*Squeak!?*"

Lilly gave Apple a shocked look.

"Look, Lilly, stairs!" said Squid in relief.

The four jumped down the trollem-size stairs through an immense stone hallway chiselled out of the very bones of the mountain. Shadows danced and flickered along the stone walls. They heard clattering and clanking, and muffled voices, and - the sound of music? Approaching a tall stone arch, they peered around its corner.

The kitchen was chaos! Fairy chefs flew through the air, twisting and turning, carrying radishes, carrots, and jugs of liquid that sloshed and slopped back into their crystal carafes. Calypso music poured from a green-and-gold singing tree that bopped away to the beat in its oversized wooden tub. Chefs called and yelled for ingredients, which were tossed to them - or more often *at* them. The chefs caught the flying food in bowls or pans or chopped them mid- flight - or else got hit in the noggin. Their knives blurred at fantastical speed, chopped veggies flying to land, diced into bowls. Dials and gadgets whistled and popped, and flavours and yummy aromas drifted on the chaotic, stirred air.

Lilly, Squid, and Tiny peered about, sniffing and sighing at all the yummy-yummy smells as they tapped their feet to the beat. There were two parts to the kitchen around the edge, tiered benches, like stadium seating, but with long curved stone benches of different heights and sizes to accommodate the multitudes of different-sized chefs; at the centre, everything was trollem-sized.

Ponderous silvered-black iron-stoves were mounted in the middle of the kitchen, and on top sat all these strange, shaped-stone pots and pans, and odd gadgets with lots of spouts, and curly glass apparatuses, weird symbols inscribed into their sides, which crackled and glowed with vibrant energy. The pots bubbled ferociously; some floated slowly, twirling above the blistering blue flames. Things whizzed and twirled as coloured smoke spurted, and the occasional lightning strike spat out from a small wandering thundercloud, accompanied by a loud ***BANNNG!***

Kitchen, the trollem was magnificent, dark, curvy, and gorgeous, her daisy apron awhirl and her chef hat tight against her brow as she bounced and shimmied to the beat, cooking with a rapt smile from ear to ear. Enormous deep sinks piled high with mountains of dishes lined parts of a wall. Buoyant soap bubbles glided about in the air, slurping-in unsuspecting fairies, who slipped and slid around inside, yabbering to be let out. Teeny purple fairies with Elvis's hair, who scrubbed and cleaned, stealing bites of food when no one was looking.

Tall, skinny fairies trundled in with wheelbarrows full of onions and peaches and netted strange white furry things that wiggled. Others carried silvered roasting dishes, balanced on top of their heads while they dodged through the mayhem on their way to Kitchen. On one silvered roasting platter lay a seven-legged creature they had seen earlier; another held great big red fish with huge eyes, and another had a single giant head of purple cauliflower surrounded by those fuzzy wiggly things. Kitchen sprinkled spices from her apron absently as they passed by; she held a jumbo wok in her hand - she flicked it and flung it as her wide hips sambaed to the funky beat. Noodles and chopped veggies flew up into the air with a flare of flame, then sloped! Back down to land in her wok.

They wondered over to her.

"Hello again!" She said with a big smile and squirted some type of sauce into the sizzling pan from a rounded, squishy, furred animal. Steam gushed and rolled about as she tossed the contents of the wok once more. Then the food flicked high up into the air. Squid watched as it flew up and up. A fairy waiter barrel- dived down from above carrying a stack of large bowls; he juggled the bowls in a circle, catching a portion of flying stir-fry in each one, then off he darted without spilling a thing.

"What can I do for you?" Kitchen bellowed as she spun around to face a vast marble-topped counter. A large ceramic pink bowl flickered into her hand. Chefs whizzed across to her, carrying ingredients. They cracked eggs and poured milk as they flew; cups of flour and a sugar bowl all went into Kitchen's overly large pink bowl. Kitchen's hand darted out, and she snatched a fairy out of the air between two large fingers and gave it a good shake: Gold dust shimmered down.

Kitchen looked at the little group.

"Tastes like spiced cinnamon."

The fairy flew off sideways and cross-eyed. Kitchen whisked the mixture, her hand a speeding blur.

"We all just wanted to say how marvellous everything is and to thank you in person," said Lilly.

"That's lovely to hear, my dear. I do like a compliment now an' again."

Kitchen pirouetted with the bowl held above her chef's hat, around the kitchen and through all the chef fairies, who barely managed to dodge out of her way, over to an immense hot griddle pan, where she poured out perfect round thick pancakes that sizzled and popped.

They followed her around as she flipped them in quick order. One after the other, they flew into the air, then back down to the sizzling pan. She flipped them again - flip, flip, flip, the pancakes landed into perfect stacks. She then flipped each stack high up into the air above. A waiter fairy flew down carrying a large jug and plates, pouring golden maple syrup mid-pancake flight, catching the pancakes.

"Still hungry at all? Maybe some blueberry strudel, coconut ice, banana split, spiced pumpkin doughnuts, pina colada pie, or maybe a lamington!"

"No, thank you, we're stuffed, and the way down was … a bit interesting," Lilly replied.

"Oh, what a shame I do like to cook."

"We were wondering if you could help us."

"What's the issue, little ones?"

"We need to get back to our ship on Short Beach, and Apple said there might be a way to the river from your kitchen."

"There would be a way, but it would be treacherous, and I would not suggest it."

“Treacherous?” asked Squid.

“Yes, little one, but in all often … seeking comes with its own dangers.”

“Danger, ha! I laugh in the face of danger: ha-ha HA. Why, I am Augie Bartholomew Kettleblack, the great ninja adventurer!”

“Yes, and I am Captain Red Lilly, sea water for blood and the waves in my eyes,” Lilly joined in, smiling.

“*SQUEAK!*” squeaked Tiny.

“Yes, you’re a lion.” Squid agreed.

“What about me?” Apple said. “Fearless in the face of danger, terrified of seagulls.”

“Together then,” said Lilly.

“Together”, the others chorused.

“The decision is yours - down the hall, second door on your left. The docks will give you access. Goodbye, little ones. I might cook for you again, Kia-ora.”

With that, she spun back to her cooking in a whirl of steam.

Chapter 8 - Docks -

They left Kitchen's kitchen and walked down the towering hallway until they came across a set of trollem-sized double-doors marked "dock access." Apple pushed at one of the very tall arched doors. His wings twirled and whirled, and he gritted his teeth with the strain as he pushed; suddenly, out it swung, and thick steam bellowed in, rolling across the hallway roof. They all peered into the gloom beyond as the steam cleared, a little apprehensive of what they might encounter. Tiny sniffed the air and bounded through the door but stopped when he realized no one had followed him. "*Squeak?*" he questioned.

Squid looked at his furry friend smiling with excitement, and followed him. Apple was still holding the door. "Could you hurry up, Lilly … this door is flippin' heavy!" he said, his wings buzzing madly.

"Soz," Lilly said and quickly walked through.

Apple let go of the door and ducked out of the way while the trollem-sized door slowly shut with a ***CLUNNK!***Glowing gloopy globs of fungus hung down from above in wet stretchy bulbous lengths, giving off an eerie luminous blue glow, which reflected off the dense and intricate tangles of copper pipes, completely covering the walls and ceiling of the spacious carved stone hallway. The tubes were cobbled together in strange, convoluted ways, protruding the rock. Some pipes were only straw thick, while others were as thick as a trollem's leg. There were giant valves or teeny-tiny ones that could be turned with just two fingers, dials and things that twirled, and big clunky gauges with mechanical numbers that lazily ticked round counting backwards.

Squid walked over to a dial that made a funny sound - *clinkered-clack-tiss, clinkered-clack-tiss.* He gave it a gentle tap. The black arrow wiggled around the dial then zipped back to the point indicating - 'Not Today' - which was good as the point next to that it read - 'Maybe?' - and the one next to that said - ***'RUN!'***

The group set off down the tunnel, following the pipes. Water trickled along the ground making the stone floor slippery; drips *dripped* and *dropped* as the valves *psst-ed* and *tsss-ed.* A yellowish light appeared in the distance through the gloom of the hallway, bobbing up and down, coming towards them: up and down it came, glowing brighter and brighter. A wheelbarrow, filled with freshly washed cabbage, trundled into view pushed by a very tall, pale skinny, red-bearded fairy wearing a head lamp. More and more fairies followed along behind him: a round one, a tall, dark one, a long-haired one, a gangly one, and a noticeably short wide one, each one of them wearing the same blue overalls and headlamps. All of them were pushing a wheelbarrow filled with fresh produce. The one at the front stopped suddenly with a look of shock. The others behind him hurriedly tried to pull up in time, but they only rammed into each other down the line, each one being knocked forward a step.

"Who the blazing hell are you lot then!? And what you doin' down here!?" the red-bearded fairy questioned.

Another fairy popped his head out from behind him, then another fairy, and another, and another; they all looked at the group.

"Oi, why-we stoppin'?"

"What's going on?"

"My feet are sore."

“Is it Thursday?”

“I smell dumplings!”

“Frank, keep your knickers on; we’ve got an obstruction,”

“Struth!”

“Obstruction, that’s against the regulations, that is.”

“Time wasters, I’ll say.”

“I’m hungry.”

“We’re on our way to the river, and Kitchen said it’s this way,” Lilly interrupted the din of voices.

“The big lady?”

“Did she say ‘kitchen’?”

“You got permission from the big lady herself, then?”

“What about my feet?”

“I’m still hungry!”

“It’s that way.”

“Yes, we did,” said Squid.

“It’s Tuesday.”

“Really?”

“*Squeak?*"

"Bit strange, in all."

"That beard's incredible; he must have grown it since birth!"

"We haven't got time for this, Muddy."

"I **do!** I smell dumplings!"

"From head to toe, it is."

"Ok, ok, jumpin' joey's, now move over and let us through, or Miss Kitchen will serve us up as an appetizer. Kia-ora." With that, their heads popped back into line, and off they trundled. As they went past, they gave little nods of their head lamps.

"Funny-looking obstructions, Muddy."

"Morning."

"Weird looking, too."

"Evening."

"That's fur, not a beard."

"What about the dumplings?!"

"You sure?"

"I think that lot's eaten too many mushrooms," said Apple.

The group walked on for a while, their footfalls echoing and bouncing off the tunnel walls. The air became sweeter as the chiselled-out, plumbed tunnel opened finally - to a lake in a cavern! The cave was STUPENDOUS and round, like some gigantic upside-down bowl with them inside. Massive stalactites hung down from the cavern roof, with weighty stalagmites breaking through the lake's waters and rising to meet them. They looked like monstrous fangs of some long-forgotten beast; some had joined together to form gigantic columns of white glistening limestone supporting the immense cavernous roof.

The lake was miles wide and far over on the other side a river, which poured into the basin. The lake waters shifted, steamed, and glistened, reflecting light from whopping-glow mushroom chandeliers growing from the cavern ceiling, lit with luminous warm yellow light. Long clusters of flowing jelly tendrils hung down from the mushrooms, swishing lazily back and forth in the stirred air, pulsating with tiny blue lights, which swarmed with spirals of shimmering glow bugs. The glow shone, illuminating the underground world below: a village of slim crooked red-stone houses and streets built on the sloping boulder-strewn lake edge. The homes were odd, people-sized at the bottom, and each floor branched into towers above, just getting smaller and more crooked. Each floor contained its own copper-railed balcony that jutted out into the air. The roofs of the houses were all sharp and pointy, with overlapping copper tiles and strangely shaped weathervanes that swivelled and turned in the breeze. Puffs of white clouds streamed out of meandering, piped chimneys, making the town's red stones wet and dark. Bronzed lamp posts lighted the town's cobbled streets.

Fairies zipped through the air, blurring up and around the houses in a blur. A mile-long wide curved stone dock sulked below the town. On it, crowds of fairies of every shape you could possibly think of shopped at the most curious twilight market you had ever seen. Quirky shops and stalls of sky-blues, ochres, and yellows were jammed and mounded one on top of another in convoluted ways sprawling along the length of the dock. Soft pastel-lit onion-shaped hovering tents of every colour were tethered above the hodgepodge market, like warm, luminous lanterns, strung together; some even spiralled around the mighty stalactites high above. Lengths of dyed cloth covered the vendor's stalls wafting and rippling whilst the tents above casually swayed with the waltzing breeze, backwards and forwards, up and down like strands of undulating kelp in a rolling sea.

The group quickly made their way to the village gates. Squid watched a fat glow bug buzzing around one of the long-lighted tendrils, which hung from a filly orange mushroom sprouting from the cavern wall. The bug suddenly became stuck to the tendril. It whizzed about trying to escape but was slowly reeled up to the awaiting mushroom above. The fungus opened its mouth as the bug was pulled closer and closer, and then - "CHOMP, CHOMP, YUM-YUMMMrrrr" - its bright blue tongue rolled out and licked its lips with a *THURLIP THUURLIP!*

Squid looked on with interest. "Predatory mushrooms, cool!" But then he realised that everyone had kept on walking. "Oi!" he called, running to catch up.

They could see fairies running along the dock, snagging crates and barrels with long hooked poles as cranes swung round. Thc workers threw ropes and nets to secure their loads as the cranes winched them high for loading. Further down the dock, fairies had hooked a large wooden tub with ropes attached and hauled it close. They watched as the crane raised it onto the pier. Loads of carrots tipped from the tub and tumbled down into wheelbarrows below. The big wooden tub was thrown back into the lake, where it landed with a generous ***SPLASH!*** Then it bobbed away, knocking against the dock as the current pushed it along. The group watched the tub being carried out away from the pier and far out into the lake, disappearing as it entered the mouth of a dark cave.

Old fairies tried their luck fishing, swinging their legs from the ancient-tilted pylons, whilst they smoked curly pipes with quick puffs and long exhales of fuchsia smoke, which twisted, furled, and sparkled around them. They baited their hooks with iridescent glow bugs; with long lazy flicks of their rods, they cast their lines out onto the rippling mirror waters.

Apple turned to the others, "Did you see where that empty tub just went? That must be the way. Nothing like a bumpy boat ride into a dark abyss to settle one's stomach, hey?"

They all turned to watch as another tub was dropped into the water with a ***SPLOSH!***

"If we run, we might just catch that tub," Squid chirped excitedly.

Lilly looked at the others … They were all smiling in excitement.

"This is crazy," she said.

They ran for it. Squid out front, Tiny close on his heels, Apple whizzing overhead, and Lilly gaining on them, down the cobblestone lane they ran. An old frizzy-haired grandma fairy with a stall selling fire-flowers jumped up with a start at the stampeding pirates. "SLOW DOWN, YOU FLAMIN' NUMBATS!" she yelled, shaking her twisted cane at them, but the pirates just laughed and ran on.

The tall, crooked buildings rose on either side of the cobbled stone lanes. Flowerpots filled with brightly iridescent glowing bulbous fungi hung everywhere, squirming with reaching tentacles. Balconies jutted from the buildings, where fairies sat talking to their friends, drinking steaming tea from petite crystal glasses as they hollered at their neighbours in high squeaky voices.

The stampeding pirates rounded a corner. There … a bloomin' café! Right in the middle of the cobblestone lane, packed with fairies munching and drinking. Squid slid as Lilly swerved around an extremely short waiter wearing a very tall hat, who screamed like a whistle at the charging pirate; his eyes rolled up into the back of his head as he promptly fainted. His laden tray flipped into the air! Bowls of liquid and what-nots flew; some of it even wiggled.

"Sorry!" shouted Lilly as she dodged around the diners.

Tiny jumped from table to table, kicking over deep bowls, flipping over plates as he galloped; tables tipped, soup gushed, and dumplings flew, as fairies fell off chairs screaming and yelling. Squid looked over his shoulder at the devastation as Apple buzzed in, flying backwards just above Squid's head. The café patrons were all covered with orange and purple soup, whilst the wiggle- dumplings were using the diversion to escape. They bounced and rolled, their multitudes of elastic legs wiggling around, making them go faster and jump higher. Customers slipped and slid, trying to catch the escapees, but some of the other fairies just looked angry; some even managed to stop sliding and slipping after their food and started chasing the pirates instead.

"Oi! YOU'RE GOING TO PAY FOR THAT!"

"LOOK AT WHAT YOU'VE BLOOMIN' DONE!"

"STREWTH, MY, DIN-DIN!"

"MARAUDING FLIPPIN' DRONGOS"

"RUN!" Apple yelled, laughing.

"SOZ!" Squid called back as he ran, a big cheeky smile spread across his face.

"*Squeak-squeak-SQUEEEEAAAK!!*" Tiny sped past Squid. Covered in soup and sprinting on all fours as fast as he could, he disappeared down a curly stone stairway. Lilly and Squid followed quickly, laughing, as they ran. Apple zoomed over the rail and down to the bottom of the stairway, catching up with Tiny, who just squeaked, "*SQUEAK!*" and ran on.

Lilly and Squid raced to the bottom of the stairs. Through the crowds, they could see the tub heading for the end of the dock. The mob chasing them got all jammed up at the top of the stairs; they were yelling something about wiggle-dumplings and blue-bug hot sauce. They shook their fists at the pirates, falling over each other as they did.

Lilly and Squid shot off, weaving in and out, under and around flying or strolling fairies. They jumped barrels around a rather large frilly-skirted moustachioed man pushing a triple-decker pram. Through the crowded boulevard, they chased that tub.

"Oi!" A fairy worker yelled and cursed at them. The dock was thick with shoppers. Squid was out front, laughing and dodging through the strange, coloured stalls as merchants spruiked their wares from piles of crates and barrels strewn with marvellous, weird stuff! Things that whizzed popped, glowed, gooed, sang, screeched, and rattled at their black-chiselled caged doors as other hawkers flew around with wares streaming behind them on buoyant tethered lines of inconceivable floating mosaic crystal lamps that sparked and crackled with energy, streamers of metallic cloth that shimmered and danced. Neanderthal budgies the size of ponies hopped and "'*YAWPED*'" along the ground, pushing through the crowd, tethered to their straining handlers. Other enterprising merchants had trained glow bugs, which pulsed neon to form intricate signs and arrows, advertising their peculiar wares to the streaming crowds passing by.

Stuff roasted, fish flipped, tangy spiced smoke permeated the air as tall black iron-and-copper cranes mounted to the stone dock swung back and forth slowly, hauling in crates and barrels. Lilly was accosted by a coffee-skinned flying pixie wearing an overly large white turban as he tried to sell her some peculiar teapot; he spoke to her in an excited quizzical voice as she ran, miming polishing the teapot and then holding up three fingers. Suddenly he smashed into another fairy, wearing a similar blue turban and selling the same-looking teapot. They circled angrily in the air and attacked, banging each other over the head with the teapots, shooting out red-and- green sparkles with every wack, kick, and bite. Lilly ran on.

Apple swooped in through the swinging cranes and around the floating tethered onion tents, trying to see where everyone was. He spotted Tiny running along, a heap of high stacked crates; still covered in purple and orange soup, he seemed to have also gained a collection of coloured scarves and a set of frilly pink ladies' underwear?!? Apple saw Lilly grab a long wooden pole leaning against a crate while she thundered through the exotic crowd.

The tub rounded the end of the dock.

Squid was nearly there, pushing his way through some over-large brightly multi-coloured, hopping, hungry *YAWPING* budgies; he rounded an old bouncing, banging converted caravan filled with green-furred clan gremlins, which were selling, fighting, eating, and smashing fungus jellies that wobbled about in their waffle cones. He still had a coupon for one of them, Squid remembered.

Out the back of the caravan was a pile of stacked crates, and there was that tub. Squid quickly bounded up the boxes and leapt - "HA, HA! Winner-winner, chicken dinner!" - from the end, landing in the wooden tub, which rocked back and forth, nearly tipping him into the lake. Tiny bounded from the stacked crates high above and soared through the air, his coloured scarves aflutter, his paws outstretched, Supermaning it, his messy black-and-white mohawk and lovely frilly pink ladies' underwear ruffling in the wind. Squid caught his chubby cross-dressing awesome friend in his arms - *Oomph!* - and got gooed with soup in the process.

Apple weaved in and out of workers carrying crates and barrels; fairies yelled at him to get out of the way, but then a dockworker stumbled, a barrel slipped and smashed, and green juice gushed everywhere. Apple weaved through the gap, then into the air, crashing into Squid and Tiny. Lilly ran around the slipping workers covered in green juice; they shook their fists at her and yelled. She looked back and called, "SORRY!" as she ran. Lilly was nearly at the end of the dock. She pelted harder and faster, lifting the long pole above her head, holding it with both hands just like she'd seen an Aussie Olympian pole-vaulters do. Just before the end of the stone dock, Lilly dipped the pole down into a crack in the stone and ***SPROING!*** Out from the pier, she sailed, the wind whistling by, and landed in the tub on top of everyone else.

"Get off … Lilly, OW!"

"You're BENDING MY WING!"

"*SQU-eak!*"

"Your foot is in my face!"

Soon, with much shoving and shouting, and a whole lot of squeaking, they got themselves sorted in the squishy tub - and, finally, they heard the outcry from the dock.

"YOU SILLY NUMSKULLS!" Fairies zipped and charged about here and there, grabbing ropes and tying them off on the dock. Some of the crowd looked on, their faces full of shock!

"DODDERING FLAMINGOS!" one shouted.

"FLAMIN', WOMBATS!" Dockworkers were trying to fly a rope out to them. They all looked so worried.

"CATCH IT, YOU DARN DRONGOS!" a fairy yelled to them. But the rope didn't reach anywhere near them.

"Maybe we should have put more thought into this?" Apple said.

One of the fairies began to yell, pointing behind them, "THERES A WATER FA …"

Then the lights went out.

Chapter 9 - Before You Leap -

The tub dropped, and down they went, tumbling through the air into the blackness.

BANG! *Splash ...*

The tub hit the bottom of the falls hard, throwing Lilly over the side and into the water. Squid, Tiny, and Apple lay battered in the bottom of the wooden tub; water poured in, sloshing over them. Apple sat up, coughing and spluttering as he felt around in the tub.

"Where's Lilly? ... Squid, Tiny ... Lilly's not here!" The tub bounced and rocked; waves smashed into the side. Water roared in the darkness as they were carried downstream, up and down, tipping back and forth, water sloshing and spraying.

"LILLY!" Squid shouted.

"LILLY!" they all yelled into the dark.

"*SQUEAK!*" squeaked Tiny - but nothing could be heard except gurgling, churning water and the loud crash of the falls.

"LILLY!!" Squid called again, with tears in his eyes.

"*Lilly*," he repeated in a small voice as he tried to peer into the blackness, his hands gripping the wooden edges of the tub.

Tiny pushed Squid out of the way and, grabbing the side of the tub, lifted his nose high into the air and sniffed and sniffed.

"*SQUEAK-SQUEAK!*" He grabbed Squid and pulled him to the other side of the tub.

"Where, Tiny, WHERE!?"

Tiny sniffed again.

"*SQUEAK!*" Tiny pushed at Squid. Squid plunged his hands over the side into the warm water. Tiny sniffed and squeaked as Squid searched frantically in the water.

Something bumped his finger.

Apple and Tiny grabbed the back of Squid's shirt, trying to keep him in the tub as he reached and reached. It was cloth! He held it and pulled,

screaming, "***PULL,*** *APPLE!* ***PULL,*** *TINY!*"

Apple's wings whirred and spun as he strained and pulled.

"*Squeak, SQUEAK, SQUEEEEAK!*"

As they pulled, they heard a gasp for breath in the darkness. Squid dragged his catch closer to the tub, wrapping his arms around her. "I GOT LILLY!" he yelled over his shoulder. He half hauled her up, and Tiny grabbed her arm and helped; Apple grabbed her collar and pulled. Squid heaved with all his strength, and together they lifted Lilly up and into the tub. They lay there wet, huffing and puffing while she gasped for breath as the tub continued ferrying them off into the darkness.

"Lilly? … Lilly?" Squid asked gently.

Then Lilly coughed and started sobbing, throwing her arms around her little brother. "Thank you, Augie, thank you."

Afterwards, they were all noticeably quiet in the tub, arms wrapped around each other with just the sound of the churning, rumbling river to keep them company. The tub spun about, tipping and sloshing, banging into rocks and the cavern walls, frightening them with every *BANG!* and *CRACK!*

On and on, they journeyed through the darkness.

Then the cavern ceiling suddenly came-alight, with hundreds and hundreds of nuggets of luminous red ruby crystals, lighting the way briefly as they looked up in amazement. The water whooshed them further and further along, leaving the red-crystal cavern far behind them. Back into the blackness, they were unhappily carried, and on they went, growing more and more frightful with each churning jolt and bump in the dark. But after a while, the river slowed and smoothed. As the blackness slowly lifted, they were able to see shapes and could see each other. They peered over the tub's edge and hoped that they had come to the end of this perilous journey.

"*Squeak.*"

"What's that?" asked Squid.

"What's what?" said Lilly.

Apple peered over the side of the wooden tub. "I see light!?!"

Lilly looked up. She could see something. "Are they *more tubs?*" Their tub slowed as it bobbed along; they were caught in an eddy of water swirling back on itself. Before them was a crowd of jostling wooden tubs, bobbing and clonking into each other. And there! A small stone dock with a crane and a ramp circling around and up to a gate and outside! “LOOK-LOOK!” Squid yelled as he pointed towards it. They burst out laughing and hugged each other in their sodden wet clothes and fur.

“Come on, guys, let’s get out of here,” said Lilly.

Apple flew up and over to the little stone dock. Tiny jumped up, bounding from tub to tub, making it look effortless. He stood on the little stone dock deciding if he should take off some of his new ‘clothing’. That left Lilly and Squid to make their way across. With a lot of advice and encouragement from Apple and Tiny and a lot of creative direction - Squid finding out that he could do the splits at one point when two tubs decided that they didn’t like each other’s company, brother and sister finally made their way onto the dock.

Tiny decided that pink just wasn’t his colour, but he kept on the orange scarf. The sodden group trudged up the ramp until they came to a sturdy wood-framed farm gate. The warm, bright sun dazzled them. They shielded their eyes with their hands and blinked as they adjusted to the bright light but were overjoyed at the wonderful smell of the open fresh air and the sight of vegetables and fields of grain stretching out into the distance.

In terrace after terrace, above and below them, giant steps were carved into the hillsides, where farm crops grew. Fairies in floppy straw hats bobbed up and down in the fields, picking carrots, pumpkins, cabbages, beets, and cauliflowers. Singing trees grew in the corners of the farmed steps, swaying majestically. The wheat fields rippled with the sea breeze as fairies flew about carrying watering cans, drizzling down long streams of water nourishing the fields below. Donkeys with little carts trundled along low, stonewalled cobblestone lanes with wooden tubs strung on their backs. Some of these tubs were full, some were empty, and there were no drivers to be seen, but the donkeys looked as though they knew where they were going.

"*EEEEE-ORRRRR ... EEEEEE-ORRRRRR!*" a donkey brayed at them.

"Fabio, what's all that racket about, what you spotted?" an old, burly fairy called as he floated up the hill, his large falcon-like wings holding him aloft; they twitched and flicked in the breeze with a mind of their own. The fairy's silver hair poked up through a large hole in his straw hat, which looked as if it had been partly munched on by something. His skin was bronzed from the sun, and his old blue jeans had seen better days; he was as weather-beaten as an old hardwood stump. Short silver hair curled up his ham-sized arms and poked out the top of his tight, faded blue singlet, a close-cut silver beard framing his face. He watched them with startling blue eyes. "Who in the fiddling fiddler are you-lot, then!?"

"We are trying to get to Short Beach," Lilly replied.

"Well, that's lovely, dear, but who are ya?" His muscles rippled in his arms, shoulders, and chest as his wings snapped angrily*!*

"I'm Lilly, that's Squid, and that's Tiny, and ... *Apple*. Squid, where's Apple?"

"Did ya say 'Apple?'" the farmer interrupted. "Little fella, glitter-punk?"

"Yes, that's him; do you know him?"

"APPLE, get out here, NOW!" the fairy barked firmly. Apple appeared, flying over the gate and landing in front of the farmer fairy. He looked like he was going to be in a heap of trouble.

“You took this lot; through there?” The fairy pointed to the gate. Apple nodded.

“You did … Floomin’ STREWTH! … Got a kangaroo loose in the top paddock, don’t ya, boy! Leading this lot that way, lucky you didn’t all come a-gutsa.”

“Sir,” Lilly ventured.

“What? No ‘sir’s around here - name’s Wayne.”

“Well … Wayne, we need to get home, and we were told that the way we came was the fastest.”

“Who told you that?”

“Kitchen.”

“Kitchen … The bloomin’ dark-bronzed goddess of a woman herself - was she cooking and dancing at the time?”

“Yes, she was,” said Lilly.

“That would be … not the best time for asking - her mind’s on … other things. She was right in one way: It *is* the quickest, but she missed telling you, as you found out, that there is a bit of a *drop.*” He sighed. “Ok, what’s done is done. Short Beach, ya say?”

“Yes, please. Can you help us?”

“Does ya mums know where you are?”

“Not the exact spot,” said Squid, as he grimaced.

“So, she hasn’t got a flamin’ clue, does she?” He eyed them with a frown, “Can’t have ya mum go all troppo. Well, we’ll see what we can do; hey, Fabio?”

“*EEEEE-ORRRRR,*” Fabio agreed.

“Looks like we’re not getting a tub after all, " Wayne said as he patted the donkey. He turned and gave the kids a warm smile. “Alright, kids, you all look like you’ve been through a damn wringer of a time. So, come on then - jump on up, squirts, and we’ll give you a lift.” They hopped up on the back of the cart, dangling their feet over the wooden sides as Fabio clip-clopped along; his hooves rang out against the cobbled stones, making music as they went.

Slowly the four companions dried out in the warm sun as they trundled along. Wayne glided in little hops and jumps next to them, his old leather boots just touching the ground, his falcon wings happily cupping the slight sea breeze alongside them. He pointed out different family terraces, telling them who farmed what as they passed. Each farmed terrace had a beautiful family singing tree that swayed in the breeze; there were lilacs, shimmering greens, mauve, and rust-coloured reds. Farming fairies flew past, giving little nods of their heads, saying, “G’day.”

Wayne said he had a quick errand to fly and would be back in a jiffy; then he looked to the sky, his large falcon wings plunged with a great ***WOOOOSSHHH!*** And he blasted off. *His hat must be glued on,* thought Squid.

“Apple, did you know what would happen to us back there?” Squid asked, looking over at him.

Apple sighed, “Nothing like that …” he said. “I mean …when your elders say don’t do this, don’t do that, don’t eat that - that’s one thing. But ‘Don’t walk under the drop-bear because he will claw your face off, tear off your wings and use your skin to make its slippers’ is another.”

“So, you didn’t know?”

“Nah … I didn’t. I didn’t think about the danger; I just thought it would be a little bit dark and a nice boat ride. Elders warn us about stuff to keep us safe, and sometimes you have to think for yourself, *…What could happen?!* There’s stuff that’s really dangerous out there,” Apple said as he stared down at the cobbled stones, thinking about how they could have lost Lilly in the dark.

Wayne swooped in, clutching a couple of bright copper pails; his wings flared open as he landed. “This will tie you over, squirts.” The buckets were filled with strawberries, blueberries, and bopple-nuts. “Thanks!” chorused Lilly and Squid.

“*Squeak,*” squeaked Tiny.

“Thanks,” Apple said quietly.

They sat munching away as Fabio plodded down the lane, fast approaching the end of their cart ride. The ocean's crash could be heard as the surf rolled off in the distance - they must be getting close.

“All right, Fabio, you beautiful animal, this looks to be a parting of our ways.” Fabio clip-clopped a little further till he came to a stone arch at the end of the lane.

“Ok, squirts, this is it,” said Wayne as he courteously helped Lilly down.

As Tiny followed, Squid leaped down onto the old stone wall. Squid looked at Apple, waiting for him. Apple looked sad.

"What's wrong?"

"You're leaving … "

"Oh, I forgot you're not coming." Squid leapt back aboard the cart and wrapped his arms around his friend. Tiny also jumped back onto the cart deck, wrapping his furry, chubby arms around them.

"*Squeak, squeak …* "

"Watch what you're doin', you darn lion," said Apple with a hiccup and a sniff. "You'll poke my eye out with a whisker." They all laughed. Lilly leaned over and gave Apple a little kiss on his head. Apple's wings blurred and whizzed as his cheeks went red. Then Apple jumped up and made a little loop-de-loop in the air.

"Thank you, Apple, for showing us your world," Lilly said.

"Hey, maybe next time you could come to my house?" asked Squid.

"That sounds like a great idea!" agreed Lilly.

"Yeah, ok." Apple smiled. "That sounds good."

"You guys are burning day-light - time to make a move," Wayne interrupted gently.

"Thanks for the lift, Fabio, and thank you, Wayne."

"No trouble at all, my pleasure. Now get home to ya mum. Goodbye, nice meeting you … Apple; I will be letting your mum and dad know what you've been up to. So, to that, I will be seeing you at my terrace tomorrow with a few hundred or so extra chores. And I believe it's that time of year for the buggle-budgies' pen to be cleared out." Wayne looked to the sky, and his falcon wings plunged with a ***WOOOOSSHH!*** He blasted off.

Squid looked on longingly. "Jeez! I wish I could do that." He stuck his arms out, pretending to fly, zooming around. Apple frowned, then shrugged and flew after Squid, laughing and having fun. Tiny jumped from the stone arch, paws outstretched, wind ruffling his fur and scarf "*Squeak!*" he chimed as he landed, running around, then doing it again.

"*EEEEEORRRRR,*" said Fabio as he plodded around to face the other way, looking over his shoulder before trundling off.

"I better be going home, too," said Apple, giving everyone a quick hug goodbye.

"I will send you a letter, 'Kay?"

"Please," said Squid.

"Bye!" Apple waved and shot off with a loud ***BANG!*** Green sparkles swirled and tinkled down, dissipating as he flew off.

"I will miss him," Squid said.

"You two will see each other again, I'd say. Tiny, nose to the wind, and lead the way!" Lilly commanded.

"*Squeak-squeak.*" squeaked Tiny as he turned and scampered up the trail, Squid not far behind him.

Lilly looked back towards the valley: majestic singing trees swaying, with their metallic pink and lavender leaves; all the terraced farms carved into the hills; rippling fields of grain, bopple- nut groves, and rows of produce. A sigh of contentment escaped her.

“Come on, Sis,” Squid called from up the trail.

“*Squeak!*”

Lilly turned with a smile on her lips and jogged after them.

Chapter 10 - Homeward -

They followed the trail as it wound its way up to the top of the hill. The sea breeze ruffled their hair as they looked out onto the Tasman Sea, with its windswept waves and blue-sapphire clear waters. Squid gazed out and thought, *home is out there somewhere*. The trail wandered down, and around the bluff and through the salt-sprayed trees, and there they found Chester. He bobbed and swayed his masts excitedly, like some happy puppy wagging his tail. The tide had come in and lifted him from the beach. They all laughed and ran down to the shore. Diving into the warm sea, they swam out to the little Spanish galleon; the rope ladder unfurled with a CLACK and *CLATTER* and climbed up. Lilly ran her hand over the polished warm honey-coloured timbers and the green-padded scaled-leather rails as she made her way up to the ship's helm.

"I've missed you, Chester," Lilly whispered as she grasped the helm; the studded leather was warm under her touch, and the little ship thrummed with pleasure.

"SQUID, TINY!" she barked, "Look lively - full canvas, tight lines. We race the sun."

"Home," Squid said.

"*Squeak,*" Tiny squeaked.

Lilly whispered to Chester, "Home," as she spun the helm, the pink polka-dot ship sails filling with a great gust of wind. Lilly's red braids whipped about her as Chester's timbers creaked, and his springs sprung as he surged through the sea. They sailed away from the island of the singing trees and headed deep out onto the Tasman Sea.

Seagulls squawked and shrilled as they hovered around in the air as Chester crashed and churned his way through the waves. Dolphins joined them in their race for home, leaping high and spinning through the air. Squid was just above them, clinging onto the bowlines, being held up by one of Chester's great clawed paws. He reached out, trying to pat one of the dolphins, getting absolutely soaked in the process.

High above in the crow's-nest, Tiny kept a sniff out, the wind ruffling his fur and scarf, his mohawk whipping about in the wind. His keen brown eyes twinkled as he searched the horizon.

"*SQUEAK,*" he squeaked.

"Right, Tiny - a little to port." Lilly corrected Chester's course.

Squid climbed back onto the deck, dripping wet, and ran up to his sister. "The dolphins just disappeared, Lilly. It was odd - they were there, and then they just weren't?"

Lilly looked out at the Tasman Sea. It had changed colour to a storm green as clouds raced overhead towards the setting sun. Hold up. The sun had not been setting a minute ago; they'd had another couple of hours at least. The wind had picked up, churning the ocean's swell. Seabirds screeched and called as they flew past, panicked - then vanished! Squid turned back to look one last time at the island, but it was gone. The night sky was there instead, with stars glimmering. Squid looked to the bow: the sun was setting, and it was still daylight, yet the night sky was behind them; *this is weird,* he thought.

Then Squid tugged on his sister's arm. "Lilly, look, the sky."

"Yeah, Squid, it's weird; the sun shouldn't be setting for ages."

"No, Lilly, look behind you."

"What?" Lilly turned around " … Oh, my!" she exclaimed. The Milky Way hung there, glistening in perfect clarity, with billions of bright, shiny stars splashed across the night sky. Galaxies swirled, planets roamed as suns ebbed and died, exploding in triumphant fire. Pastel colours smeared the night sky - from midnight blues to clouds of powered ice and sprays of burnt orange, blazed behind their little ship.

"*SQUEAK-SQUEAK!*"

Lilly and Squid quickly spun around. A coral reef jutted from the ocean; water washed down its sides.

"I see it, Tiny!" Lilly called back as she spun the ship's helm hard to starboard. Chester swayed, tilting heavily; his carved, ridged boom swept across dangerously, just above their heads, whipping over from port to starboard. Squid went toppling across the deck, slamming into the rail, his arms and feet dangling over the edge just above the rushing water. The great sails relaxed hung limp, and then cracked full of the rushing wind. Chester surged around the exposed reef as Lilly spun the ship's helm back, righting the vessel again. Jagged stone outcrops broke through the surface of the Tasman Sea as it rushed them towards the setting sun. Lilly spun the helm in one direction, then quickly back, weaving Chester in and out of the exposed rock, keeping the little ship from being torn apart. Lilly looked worried but determined as she called out,

"Squid, run a safety line from the mast to each of us, quick!"

"Gotcha, sis!" He hurried across the deck and down the stairs, his bare feet slapping against the wet leather. Chester heaved from side to side as the boom creaked and groaned, swinging back and forth. Chester plunged down a deep ocean trough, and all they could see was water; down, down, they went; Squid slipped and slid all the way to the thick curved tree-mast as the ocean rolled towards them; then up they came, bursting over the rolling swell.

Whitestone cliffs rose out of nowhere before them, with a tremendous jagged crack running down its centre. The sea ploughed into the fracture, tearing its way through. Waves crashed; the ocean groaned as the wind drove them towards the cliffs.

"I CAN'T GO AROUND; WE HAVE TO GO IN!" yelled Lilly over the churning crash of the pounding surf.

The sea poured into the crack in the cliff, taking them with it.

The power of the waves was immense as they tore their way through. Squid grabbed a line from the mast and tied it quickly to his waist, holding another line for Lilly; he took off through the sloshing water and ran up the stairs. Chester bucked and heaved, nearly knocking Squid off his feet. Lilly caught him with one hand and held him up - it was like she was welded to the deck. He tied a line around her waist, wiping saltwater from his eyes.

Chester's hull scraped and ground against the crumbling rock walls as protruding serrated stone tore at the pink polka-dot sails. The long wooden boom swung out, grinding against the cliff face, tearing chunks from its timbers whilst water bulged around them, heaving them on; broken rock crashed from above, snapping rigging and marring the scaled-leather deck. Lilly was masterful on the wheel, spinning it back and forth as Chester surged and fell through the tumultuous chasm.

"SQUEAK!"

Squid looked up. Tiny was still at the top of the mast, in the crow's-nest, barely hanging on as he was thrown around, trying to give warnings of oncoming danger. Squid let go of Lilly and ran down the stairs, across the wet leather, and straight over to the mast. He coiled up a safety line and looked up. The vine rigging was mangled, and the mast swung wildly as Chester bucked and heaved. Squid grabbed the rail, and up he climbed. Cliffs of stone raced past on either side of them; one false move from Lilly at the ship's helm would mean a smashed, ground, splintered death for them all. Wind, water, and noise hammered at him as he climbed; his hands were cold and sore.

Chester hit a massive outcrop of stone, and his keel ground against the rock, tilting the ship sideways; Chester's great scaly clawed paws dug into the stone, hauling them on as his strong elephant feet pushed and heaved. Squid held the lines tightly as he swung out, dangling in the air. Tiny looked down from above. *"SQUEAK!"* An overhang of fractured rock jutted out from the oncoming ravine wall and was charging at him - Squid was about to come to a sudden … stop - smashed to bits like a bug against a car's windscreen.

Squid swayed back, then forwards, and then leapt through the air. His arms windmilled, he caught a vine and swung - and just … stopped - His face centimetres from the opposing wall of fractured, grinding death.

"*Squeak,*" Tiny called. Squid felt pain; he hung there, holding on, but he had to get up to Tiny somehow. Tattered vines dangled down - he reached out and grabbed one, wrapping it around his wrist as Chester powered on through the raging white water. He struggled but managed to pull himself up and up, climbing what was left of the remaining rigging. At last, he fell into the flowering bristled crow's nest.

Tiny squeaked in relief as Squid rolled over and up onto his knees, tying the line around Tiny's waist with his sore and raw hands. Then Chester sploshed out of the canyon onto a tumbling white-churning sea. Seaspray was thick in the air. Squid and Tiny looked out from the crow's-nest at the raging disintegrating world.

Lilly called up to them. "WHAT DO YOU SEE?"

In every direction they looked, the ocean was being slowly tipped out, as if they were on some planet-sized plate, white water smashed and spewed, rolling ever onward towards an edge. It was the edge of everything - there was no going back, there was no going forward, there was just … nothing left.

A sliver of the sun could be seen: its rays of light shot through the boiling black clouds as beautiful, impassive twinkling stars shone in the background, calmly observing the world's destruction. Squid searched frantically in every direction for something - anything! - just to give them a chance. Tiny sniffed and sniffed, but nothing - just more raging churning-white sea.

Squid grabbed Tiny, hugged him close, and then turned and called down to Lilly in a worried voice, "It's all coming apart! There's just gimassive falls to nowhere!"

Lilly spun the helm and cut Chester across the raging current, their battered little ship doing his best. Lilly didn't say anything; she just looked Squid in the eye for a second, then cut Chester back to starboard, zigzagging back and forth to fight for time. But they were still carried inevitably to the edge. Lilly was quiet, grim determination on her face as her mind raced for a way to save them.

Everything she came up with wouldn't work. If they dropped anchor and it caught, the pressure of the water was moving so fast that the chain would snap - or Chester would go under, or they would be torn apart. There were no islands or even a darn big rock to tie up to, just churning white water.

Damn it, she thought. The flippin' story had come to an end. A smile bloomed on her face with relief. She looked up to Squid and Tiny.

"Hey, you two, it's the end!" she called up happily.

"What?" Squid called back.

"*Squeak?*"

"The end, Squid, it's the end," she repeated.

"You've gone barking mad, Sis - we're about to sail over the most gimassive waterfall ever! We will be smashed, cracked, dismembered goo, splattered all over who knows what!"

"*Squeak-SQUEAK-squeak.*" Tiny chimed in.

"Yeah, what he said - there's no-way-out, Sis."

"There is a way, Squid; it's just stupid scary. The end is here, Squid. *IT'S TIME TO GO HOME!*" she yelled as she spun the helm. Chester stopped his zigzagging course against the raging tsunami and headed straight for the falls. The brave ship skipped and bounced, his vine rigging in tatters, their pink polka-dot sails holed and ripped but still taut and strong. His hull was scraped and chipped, his railings battered and broken, deep gouges marred his timbers. Lilly laughed hysterically, "*MaWhaHA-HHARR,*" her hands firm on Chester's helm as the end of this world came up fast and furious. Storm clouds raged; salt spray stung their eyes as the grinding roar of a dying world deafened them. Squid and Tiny yelled as they launched over the world-ending falls to nowhere …

“*SQUUUEEEEEEEEAKKK!*”

“*AHHHHHHHHHHHHHHHHH!*”

“*MaWhaHA-MaWhaHAHhAR!*”

Chapter 11 - Somewhere, Maybe? -

The wind whistled in their ears and tore at their clothes as sea spray blinded them all. Squid and Tiny held onto each other and yelled and yelled and yelled and … yelled? Squid started to get bored of all this yelling - "AHHHHHErha … ?" -as the wind grew silent.

He opened his eyes.

Giant wobbly globs of water and stars were above them, below them, surrounding them, jiggling and contorting, slurping together and then slurping apart like gimassive balls of gelatinous wiggling gooey jelly. Tiny lifted into the air beside him, floating?! His eyes squeezed tightly shut, and his body all tensed; Squid also started to rise. He quickly grabbed the edge of the crow's-nest and held on. They weren't plummeting to their deaths; they were flamin' floatin'! Squid grabbed Tiny's lifeline and reeled him back in. Holding onto his friend, he said, "Tiny, open your eyes."

Tiny shook his scruffy-furred head.

"*Squeak,*" he squeaked in protest.

"Tiny, seriously, you've got to see this!"

Tiny slowly opened one eye, then the other, and his eyes grew larger as he looked around. "*Squeak-Squeakily-Squeak!*" he said.

"Yeah, bloomin'-oaf, I know," replied Squid.

Lilly floated up to the crow's nest behind them, her hands on her hips and a big smile on her smug face. Her long red braids floated out and about her captain's hat. "Hey, boys, we're not dead!" she stated gleefully.

"*Squeakily, squeak,*" said Tiny.

"Yeah! Where are we, Lilly?"

"We're *somewhere*," Lilly said seriously as she looked about. "Or maybe nowhere - depends, really, on your point of view."

"You haven't got a bloomin' idea, do ya, Sis," Squid stated.

"Nope. Haven't got a flippin' clue, squirt, but check this out," Lilly said happily as she kicked off the crow's-nest and did a lazy triple back somersault just like an astronaut in space. Her lifeline floated out behind her, and Lilly grabbed it, slowing her spins till she stopped and reeled herself back in. Her red braids waving about as if underwater, she smiled at the boys encouragingly.

"Cool!" said Squid.

"*Squeak!*" seconded Tiny.

"We're in space!" Squid cried.

"Don't know if it's space - we are still breathin', and we aren't frozen solid. Chester doesn't seem to be moving. ... Or maybe we are, and it's just that those surrounding stars are so far away that we just can't tell."

Tiny pushed off from Squid slowly, with his paws outstretched, showing off his chubby white furry belly as he slowly swam through the air with lazy guineapig breaststrokes. "*Squeakily squeak, squeak, squeak,*" he squeaked happily.

Squid floated out, a little apprehensive at first, then the realisation hit him that he was flamin' flying, floating - awesomeness. He flipped upside down, floating like a balloon on a string, then yanked his lifeline and shot down to Chester's crocodile-scaled padded deck like a dive-bombing magpie, where he spun around mid- dive, landing on his feet, and then sprang back up to the others - *BOING!* "YEAH!" he called excitedly.

Lilly floated lazily in the air, playing with shimmering, cohesive wobbly water droplets she had collected. She rolled them around on her fingers and along her arms as they glooped and globbed. The droplets split and slurped back together convulsively:it looked kinda alive. Tiny came slowly cartwheeling across. He smiled happily at them as his head came round, and round, and round, and round, and round.

Lilly gazed up at a star much brighter than the others as Tiny and Squid floated far above Chester's deck, playing.

"Hey, Squid, look at that star."

Squid stopped spinning and flipping, pushing off the curved mast tip and gliding through the air to Lilly.

"Look at what?"

"That star, there,"

"Oh, that one."

"*Squeakily squeak.*"

"Yeah, you're right; it is kinda bluish." Lilly shook the globular droplets from her fingers, and they flicked off in all directions – suddenly, they curved up, taking off towards the blue star. All around them, the wobbly goblets of gloopy water, large and small ***ZIP! ZIP! ZIPPED!*** Off in a blink of an eye.

Gravity returned. Squid, Tiny, and Lilly dropped! Falling, they all slammed and bounced off Chester's padded leather deck. *BOING, BOING, BOING,* they bounced.

"*Squeak-ek.*"

BOING.

"This is kinda,"

BOING.

"Fun!"

BOING.

"Yeah!"

BOING.

"I think,"

BOING.

"We're,"

BOING.

"Moving!"

BOING.

"*Squeakily!*"

BOING-BOING-BOING, doing-doinng-doinng.

Their bouncing came to a stop; Chester vibrated, his timbers groaned, as his ship sails suddenly shrunk, smaller and smaller, as his ragged rigging and vine ladders were all sucked into the mast with one big, long ….

SLUUUUUUURRRRRRRRRP-PA!

Chester's scaled-leather deck rippled and crackled and crinkled. The ends of the little ship abruptly popped shorter and shorter. The tree-mast whipped back and forth as bristled fronds closed up over the crow's-nest , and the mast shrank down and down, smaller and smaller, back to its former broomstick self. The ship cannons ***CRACKED!*** Back into cushions, bouncing and rolling about.

Railings folded, stairs flipped and clunked Chester wiggled; the leather deck rolled and lifted them off their feet, then sat them down on Chester's lumpy, bumpy padded cushions. The back rail sucked in, forming the backrest, flinging Nanna-Nan's pillows on top of them. Chester's port and bow rolled back into his original curved, buttoned, crocodile-scaled armrests - he was back to being a couch. His sharp prehistoric scaled, clawed paws stretched forward, clasping at the air; his stompy African elephant feet kicked out at the back.

Stars zipped by.

The broomstick mast, poking out of Chester's middle, bent and quivered in the onrushing cyclonic winds. Their pink polka-dot bedsheet streamed out, thrashing behind them. The wind buffeted them; faster and faster, they sped through space on their lumpy, bumpy couch.

Lilly wrapped her arm around her little brother as Squid held Tiny tight. Their clothes wriggled and wiggled, morphing back. Lilly's captain's hat flicked off. She tried to catch it, but it had whipped back into the depths of space - lost. White clouds surged around them, pelting them with cold, wet air; their eyes squeezed shut as they hurtled along at ferocious speed …

"ARRRRRUUUUGGGGHHHHHH!"

"SQUUUUEEEEEAAAAKKKKKK!"

"ARRRRUUUUUGGGGGHHHHH!"

BAAANNNG!!!

They smashed into their lounge room, their lamp falling over and hitting the floor. Lilly and Squid tumbled onto the rug and lay there panting, trying to catch their breath. Squid lifted his head and looked around - they were home.

Squid got up slowly. With a warm smile, he walked over to the fallen lamp, picked it up and put it back on the doily-covered side table next to Chester. He ran his hand over the couch's crocodile-scaled leather, feeling Chester's warmth. Lilly sat up and smiled at her little brother. Chester looked just how he always looked; old and a bit slanted; chunky life-sized elephant feet at the back, big prehistoric scaly clawed paws at the front; lumpy, bumpy, and comfy, with his strange-buttoned, bulging, green crocodile-scaled shiny leather.

Maybe Chester had a little-bit more character here and there, perhaps a few more scrapes and scratches on his swirling carved honey-coloured timbers. The broomstick mast back to its broomstick self, standing tall, propped in the corner with Lilly's pink polka-dot bedsheet back in one piece, still knotted to the bristled broom. Nanna-Nans crazy-coloured cushions were all there, too, scattered about the loungeroom floor. The house was fine: no Tasman Sea, the storm had cleared, and warm sunshine shone through their old farmhouse's windows. Tiny was sound asleep on Chester, with his little orange scarf still on, back to his usual fat guineapig self. His furry feet kicked in the air as he snored, dreaming some guineapig dream, "*Squeak,* ***snore,*** *squeak,* ***snore.***"

"I wonder how he fell asleep through *that?*" Squid exclaimed.

"***EEEEEEEEEEEEEEEKKK!***"

"Mum's home!" Lilly and Squid said together.

"Darn, that blue-tongue lizard - thought it was a flamin' snake! Kids, come and give me a hand with the shopping, will ya?"

Lilly and Squid ran through the house, pushing, shoving, and laughing as they banged through the old fly-screen door.

"Mum, we were on the Tasman Sea, and you got to see the zucchini and golden squash I got for dinner!" called Squid.

The End

The next morning …

CRACK … BANG!

"I'M HOME … Where the flip is everybody?"

"Bloomin', have to bring in my own bags and junk, even brought back a souvenir or two. You here, fleabag? And what about you, fur-ball?"

ThumpThumpThumpThumpThump …

Chester's elephant foot pounded the floorboards in excitement.

"*Squeak! Squeak!*" Tiny came running down the hall.

"At least Tiny and my couch are here, I'll just put this down in my room, and I'll tell ya all about my trip." Nanna-Nan took off her cherry-red winged sunglasses and shook out her long mane of purple wavy hair. "What's that I smell?? OOo-ah?! Is that *witchery* I smell?" *SNIFF-SNIFF.* "Bush-mint", *SNIFF*, "lemon myrtle," *SNIFF,* "eucalyptus - that little squirt's come of age. Ha-ha! About flippin' time. In that case, fur-ball, take the bags." Nanna-Nan chucked her bags to Tiny; they spun end over end, getting smaller and smaller as they flew through the air. Tiny leapt up and caught them, his orange scarf fluttering.

"*Squeak?*"

"Yeah, just on the end of my bed, would you, love?" Nanna-Nan walked then skipped and twirled as she danced her way down the hallway, her yellow floral dress and light-blue knitted cardigan swirling, her red saltwater-croc high heels tapping lightly away on the hardwood floorboards, all the way to Chester. "Ah, Chester, did you miss me?" she said, smiling and running her hand across his warm leather, giving him a good scratch. "Who's been a good boy then? Did you do a good job? *Aww,* such a good boy!"

ThumpThumpThumpThump!

Chester's elephant foot thumped the floor as he rolled to his side for a belly rub. "Aww, you want a belly scratch? Oooh, is that the spot? Yeah, good boy, good boy. Here, I saved you a slice of Hawaiian pizza - sit, siiiit, SIT!"

Chester rolled back and sat attentively, wiggling back and forth excitedly. Nanna-Nan stuck her hand deep into one of her oversized cardigan pockets and pulled out a rolled-up slice of pizza. "Wait for it, wait for it, and ***GO!***" She threw the piece into the air - Chester leapt! His centre cushion lifted and then slammed down, gobbling up the pizza slice as he landed back on the floor with a **THUDD!** You could see his cushions moving around as he chewed, then with a ***GULP*** and a ***BURP!*** It was gone.

Nanna-nan turned gracefully and leapt into the air, hovering, then slowly floated down to sit on her couch with great decorum, smoothing her dress over her knees and straightening her knitted cardigan.

"Now, tell me, what's been happening?"

Chester's right paw grabbed the rug and tossed it over the coffee table to give himself room. As his left foreclaw flicked out, scratching into the hardwood floorboards and tearing into the timbers, Nanna-Nan leaned forward and peered down at what he had written.

THE BOY'S VEINS RUN TRUE

As Nanna-Nan read, the timber floorboards healed, the letters disappearing. "Yes, yes, no surprise there."

Chester's claw scratched again.

HE BEFRIENDED A FAE, A GLITTER-PUNK

"Well, yes, it's Squid! He could make friends with a funnel-web spider! But what power does he have??"

NONE WAS PROCLAIMED.
DANGER WAS NOT - ENOUGH

"Lilly is too soft on the boy. You can't mollycoddle him - it makes us all too vulnerable. Well, we hid this long, waiting for him to come of age, might as well hide a little longer." Then Nanna-Nan hollered,

"HEY, FUR-BALL, WHEN'S THE NEXT SCHOOL HOLIDAYS??"

"*Squeak.*"

"Strewth! Where did you come from? You better not have been playing with that shrunken head! That's Squid's present from Peru - cost me one of my turquoise lace petticoats, that did. I must admit that chieftain looked better in it than me. Gosh, that man had killer legs, and when those jungle drums kicked up a notch, he was surprisingly light on his feet for such a muscular man."

"*Squeak, squeak, squeakily ... squeak?*"

"Around winter, school holidays are, you say. Look, don't worry your little furry head about Squid. I'll look after him. He just needs … more of a push; it took his mum a while, too, if I remember right. We're up far-north Queensland on an educational journey when she was around Squid's age, I think, and she wandered off or somethin'. When I found her, she was being slowly devoured by this humongous scrub python, stuck deep down inside its gullet she was, when all of a sudden, the bloomin' snake started swellin' up, like it was being pumped up full of air. You should have seen the look on its face when ***BANG!*** It exploded, and chunks of snake rained down all over the place. And there was my baby girl all magicked up, glow'n and stuff, covered in snake guts. *Aww,* good times." Nanna-Nan looked around and tapped her high-heel shoe against the floor, thinking, "Well, no one's home; might as well pop over and see Wayne, let him know I'm back and remind that beautiful, feathered man that I'm still single and ready to mingle. Hop up, Tiny, so we don't lose half of ya." Tiny hopped up into Nanna-Nan's awaiting arms. "Chester, Wayne's loungeroom, please, next to the steam radiator, make that loud *POP!* Noise when you do. I love making that spunky-hunky man jump."

Chester leapt into the air with Nanna-Nan and Tiny, folding them into himself with sudden jerks and twists. The couch bent and crimped as huge unseen hands seemed to crush him, making him smaller and smaller with every snap compression, until just a single heavy dark-green leather-backed ridged scale was left hanging in the air, slowly revolving. It fell, striking the ground with a loud ***TING!*** and bounced, twisting, and turning, going higher and higher, gleaming in the light. It grew brighter and brighter till it burst into emerald-green radiant flames, then disappeared into complete nothingness with a fiery *FSSST!* …

As the thin whisp of smoke dissipated at their departure, all was quiet in the old buttercup-yellow, corrugated-tin farmhouse as it awaited its family's return.

Glossary

Apple. A kid-sized, green-skinned fairy or Fae creature, known as a glitter-punk, of indeterminate age - could be ten or a hundred and ten. Wears a lot of black leather, covered in rainbow spikes and silver chains. Has his orange hair gooed up in spikes, and seriously loves punk rock, calypso, metal, with a dash of Queen - and for those moments when nothing will just hit *that* spot, Cab Calloway.

Bloomin. An expression of surprise or excitement.

Bludging, bludger. Lazy person, or a do-nothing.

Blue-Mountains. A rugged region west of Sydney in New South Wales, Australia, is known for its blue colouration. This is due to the densely populated oil-bearing eucalyptus trees filling the atmosphere with finely dispersed droplets of oil, which is a combination of dust and water particles scattering short- wavelengths of light, causing this blue-colour phenomenon, which looks really cool.

Bopple nuts. Known around the world as the macadamia nut, these nuts are indigenous to Queensland Australia, where they are also known under the name of 'Bauple nut' or 'Bopple nut' after Mount Bauple near Gympie, where they were first farmed.

Buggle-budgies. A Strange cross-bred species of the small native brightly coloured Australian parrot, the budgerigar. Having been bred back to resemble its much, much larger prehistoric fore- parents, it is around the size of a small horse or pony. It can only fly short distances and is more of a ground-dweller, living in dens or burrows. Its eggs are highly sought after, as they have the consistency of triple-thick vanilla custard and a yoke of maple-syrup-cinnamon goo.

Bus-vaulting rubbertastic fern. A plant, endemic to the singing tree island, which has extraordinary elastic capabilities. Can be used in numerous applications detached. The only way this plant can be transplanted is by coaxing it out of the ground with fermented fish marshmallows and then bedding it with star blooms in a new suitable, usable locations.

Chester. A bewitched three-seater Chesterfield couch, who is occasionally grumpy and has a fondness for slices of Hawaiian pizza. Part African elephant and something from a time that was before, he has large blue-black-green scales and oversized clawed paws, he is also extraordinarily squishy-comfy and loving of his Aussie family.

Crikey. An expression of surprise - and a big thanks to Steve Irwin, who made this saying known throughout the realms.

Daria. A 3-ish-foot-tall female fairy or Fae creature with long purple wavy hair. She loves sparkly dresses if she also wears her big, chunky, black-buckled boots. She is the lead guitarist of the Fae famous rock band 'The Red Daisey's and has a thing for dramatic power slides while wearing her grandfather's leather pilot goggles.

Drongo. A mild form of insult, which means "silly person". So-called after, a racehorse that never actually won a race, back in the 1920s, called Spangled Drongo.

Drop bear. A much, much larger, and hungrier species of koala, (which is a *marsupial,* not a bear, though it looks like a bear). Known for its beautiful sky-blue-and-grey striped fur and its never- ending carnivorous appetite. Will wait days and days high up in the eucalyptus trees perfectly camouflaged against the blue sky above, awaiting passing prey walking below. The drop bear then bungee's down silently, grabs hold of the unsuspecting victim, and disappears back to the treetops above … where it hungrily devours its prey and adds to its collection of slippers.

Fabio. A devastatingly beautiful donkey that happily helps with the pulling of farm carts for the endless supplies of carrots, apples - and any vegetable or passing hat that he can get his teeth into.

Fae / Fairy. Strange, mysterious creatures /peoples that have roamed the earth since its birth. Always where you wouldn't think, always in places you wouldn't believe, true to themselves and understand way more than you could possibly know.

Flippin', Flip, Fluming. An expression used to emphasise whatever is being said. E.g., "That was flippin' awesome," "Flippin' really?" and "What the Flip?". Not swearing, really - just Aussie.

Funnel-web spider. Known for its liking of people's shoes or boots. Causing Australians to perform themorning banging-of-footwear-on-the-ground-or-walls ritual before placing them upon one's feet. This black, hairy fanged beastie holds the grand title of one of the world's most venomous spiders.

Gimassive. This is what you get when you take *giant* and *massive* and jam them together. Meaning really, really big. A word created by my wonderful spectrum son.

Glitter-punk. A style, a reality, an external sense of self. A statement of who you are and what you are. The truth of music and all it entails - and looking badass while doing it.

Great Barrier Reef. One of Australia's greatest natural phenomena. A truly magnificent kaleidoscope of humongous creatures and organisms in one epicentre. Breeding and nursery ground for an unbelievable amount of earth's saltwater creatures, from phytoplankton to humpback whales to things that slither and fly.

Gutsa. Referring to an incident in which someone has hurt themselves badly and where stupidity was involved.

Heebie-jeebies. To make your skin crawl and get all nervous with fear and anxiety.

Kangaroo loose in the top paddock. To be crazy; to act, think, or behave in an eccentric, foolish, or nonsensical manner.

Kia-ora. A warm and welcoming greeting, which you'll hear throughout New Zealand. Comes from the indigenous Māori language and means you acknowledge not just them but everything about them, including where they come from. Pronounced "*Kee-Aura*" (roll the "r" on the tongue).

Kitchen. A beautiful trollem lady with unsurpassed culinary skill, honed through years and years of cooking trespassing pirates until finally she branched out and found other ingredients. And with this epiphanic moment, the cooking world trembled at her brilliance and fell in love with her uncanny pairings of gloopy and crunchy, and of things that zinged, and stuff that wiggled.

Kitchen's. Kitchen's kitchen. World-famous subterranean Fae restaurant. Floor after floor of soft-fungus-lighted atmosphere. Bringing the realm's top musical performers from around … well, everywhere, to entertain the astounded diners. A place where you can literally order anything that your stomach, or stomachs, desire.

Note: I suggest just asking for the daily special and see what turns up.

Kookaburra. Native bird of Australia. The largest in the kingfisher species, known for its haunting laughter/call, is used in iconic movies such as *Indiana Jones* and *the Raiders of the Lost Ark* opening scene. You know - when the birds fly out of the mouth of the statue, and stuff gets all tense and a little *!?!?!*

Leprechauns. Red furry four-foot-tall gold-obsessed creatures that wear tall black hats and emerald-green clothing with black buckled clogs. Leprechauns hate to do anything but play with their gold or find more gold or just sit back and think about *GOLD*. They will quite happily enslave any person or thing that they can to do all those other jobs, like laundry and cooking and bathing, brushing one's teeth and flying kites and feeding oneself, and all the stuff that doesn't involve their favourite and only obsession, gold!

Lilly. Lilly Ann KettleBlack. An Aussie lass who cares greatly for her strange mystical family. Loves the sea and high-powered motorcycles and mixed martial arts, which are taught to her by Phil, whose family owns the local Asian restaurant. She wants to sail this and the Fae worlds by yacht and see all the wonders they both have to offer.

Milky Way. The galaxy that contains our solar system. The name describes the sight of our solar system from the earth, a milky glittering star band spanning the night sky. A true breathtaking twinkly reality when seen from Ben Boyd National Park, down south New South Wales, which lies beside the beautiful sapphire, ever-watching Tasman Sea.

Nanna-Nan. A firecracker of a woman who has done and seen things that would blow your mind. A stunningly handsome older woman, she crackles with exuberance and playfulness and has a laugh that is loud and infectious. She just so happens also to be an outstanding dancer.

Numskull. An extremely foolish person. Or after the Fae creature who only drinks upside down when underwater.

Queen of Fae. An eternal being or god, the earth-mother, savage and delightful.

Short Beach. One of the only landing sites on the singing-tree island, a beautiful small cove of blissful white sand and sapphire clear waters.

Singing trees. Barked in chunks of organic silver and leaves of glazed steel. Each tree has its own musical soul, shown through the colour of its leaves, and expresses this when touched or when the mood takes them.

Squid. Augie Bartholomew KettleBlack, is a ten-year-old Aussie lad, who sees the world in ways that most don't, and who has an incredibly good time while doing it. Loves his family and Australia and all its animals and plants and slugs and bugs fiercely. Sometimes he finds this world hard to understand and its people strange, but he's finding his way.

Squirt, Squirts. Everyday Aussie slang referring to a child or kid, but also a sea plant/animal, named "cunjevoi" or "sea squirt". Found down by the sea edge, attached to rocks at low tide, will squirt water when stepped on, causing the above trespasser a quick, cold, wet shock.

Stalactites. A tapering structure, like an icicle, is attached to the **roof.** Forming over time through the slow deposits of calcium salts by the slow constant drip of water.

Stalagmites. A tapering structure, like an icicle, is attached to the **floor.** Forming over time through the slow deposits of calcium salts by the slow constant drip of water.

Strewth. Used to express surprise or dismay.

Soz. The shortened version of sorry.

Tasman Sea. A marginal sea in the South Pacific Ocean between Australia and New Zealand, also known as the "Ditch", e.g., "crossing the ditch", means to travel from New Zealand to Australia or vice versa.

The Docks. A Fae subterranean town. It is known for its market of softly lit balloon tents and rippling-cloth stalls and the freshest produce from all around. One of its major drawcards is its famous local cuisine of wiggle dumplings in blue-bug hot sauce.

Tinkle puff. Seeds of the great singing trees, their glowing forms float upon the wind-stirred breeze, little lives of every shape and colour ready to sprout and grow.

Tiny. Squid's pet black-and-white guineapig and close friend. Has a powerful sense of smell and a highly expressive way with squeaks.

Trollem. A humongous humanoid-like creature, ranging in forms. A protector and carer of the singing trees, who has a fondness for topiary and landscape design and will happily snack on pirates any chance they get.

Troppo. To go crazy or mad.

Wayne. An Aussie Fae farmer, strong as a bull and sharp as a tack, can fly like Luke Skywalker but without the X-wing. A really nice guy, but don't get on the wrong side of him.

Wiggle dumplings. The tasty, delectable larvae of the cavern-dwelling glow bug. The egg-sized white round body is covered in hundreds and hundreds of little elastic white legs, which can propel this creature faster and faster and bounce higher and higher in escaping predators, such as hungry diners armed with bottles of blue-bug hot sauce.

Wringer. 'Gone through the wringer' is an old term that means a person has had an exceedingly difficult or unpleasant time.

Biography of Jonathon A McDonald

G'day. I'm an author /artist /dad / Aussie / nature lover / gardener / cook.

And I like Ducks.

-Note From Author – (well, *me*)

And now, a little about myself. I wanted to let children and people know that I wasn't a writer before this, and as I hadn't obtained any form of higher education, I never thought that I could even possibly contemplate the prospect of being a writer; before pursuing this epically hard grind of an incredible adult-leaning journey. Writing in any form had been quite terrifying - I could hardly spell or use 'grammar,' and I always missed words in sentences. So, I learned to rely heavily on technology to help me with simple things such as spelling certain words: I would type a mash of letters into the Google search bar, approximating the word I was trying to spell, and then PRESTO! There was a word in its miraculous form that could convey my strange, odd, or simple views of the world.

Not being able to write has hampered my life significantly, and experiencing fear and feeling incapable is a tremendous burden. I do not wish that on anybody. But sometimes inspiration comes from the unlikeliest of places, as it did for me when I watched the excellent Australia-inspired movie *Finding Nemo,* specifically the delightful character named Dory. She has this saying, more like a philosophy, 'Just keep swimming', three such simple words, but it has helped me over so many hurdles: when I have found things just so hard, so unattainable, so beyond me.

At these times, a picture would form in my mind of this little blue fish who had her life challenges, holding the fin of her friend, supporting them both as they swam down into the darkness, singing, laughing out loud; those three truly fine words and all is made possible. So, for those of any age with their mountains, chasms, and fears before them, remember, "JUST KEEP SWIMMING".

Review & Follow Me for New Books & Aussie Stuff!

Hello to all my readers and fellow adventure-fantasy fans the world over.

Please review my stuff!

Did you like it?

Was it fun?

Was it like anything else that you have read?

Did you laugh?

Did you cry?

Did it make you hungry?

Have you been 'Aussiefied?'

Please let me know because I want to know. So here are the links; tell me and everyone else!

And thank you to you all.

Yours *BLOOMIN'!* Sincerely Jonathon A McDonald

From indie publisher Waltzing Wombats.

www.ingramcontent.com/pod-product-compliance
Lightning Source LLC
Chambersburg PA
CBHW030414310726
48979CB00002B/408

* 9 7 8 0 6 4 8 7 9 6 1 5 2 *